THE

GHOSTLY ADVENTURES

OF JAMIE C. O'HARE

~

THE CHURCH TOWER

C. Wade Jacobs

Cover illustration by A

MONKEYBAR
BOOKS

www.monkeybarbooks.com

Issued in print and in electronic formats.

ISBN: 978-1-7752211-1-1

Book design and cover by September Media Inc.

Monkey Bar Books Inc.

For J.M.M.S and J.W.S,
the inspirations for this book.

To Josh, until we meet again.
Love always, Mom xoxo

Professional Reviews

The Ghostly Adventures of Jamie C. O'Hare:

The Church Tower is a good old-fashioned ghost story in the best tradition of old-fashioned ghost stories. From a sleepy old historic town, past secrets, and a protagonist fighting grief and loneliness, the story has everything a reader needs for suspense and excitement. The main character is believable and sympathetic, and readers are sure to empathize with the everyday problems he faces besides the supernatural nightmares and ghosts. While the story is scary enough to keep the plot moving, it also ends on an uplifting note and is a reminder that sometimes change can be for the better. The Ghostly Adventures of Jamie C. O'Hare: The Church Tower is a solid start to what looks like a fun new series.

~ Children's Book Review

....

The Church Tower is a fast-paced mystery with thrilling twists and turns that are sure to keep you on the edge of your chair! Young readers will definitely enjoy this story that is packed with adventure, suspense, mystery, and thrills. Jacobs did an amazing job on the characters. They were all very different and believable. I found myself rooting for the "good guys" and wanting to stand up to the bullies. C. Wade Jacobs' The Ghostly Adventures of Jamie C. O'Hare is a quick read that I thoroughly enjoyed, and I hope to read more adventures with Jamie and his friends.

~ Readers' Favorite

KID REVIEWS

I would give every star in the universe (in all seriousness I give it a 5 star) this book is so exciting for me.

~ TOMMY

I like this book because it gives you mystery like what the ghost wants and why. I have nothing bad to say about the book because I really liked it. I would give the book a 4 star rating.

~ NAOMI P.

I would give it 5/5 because it is very on edge and makes me want to read more.

~ LUELLA S.

The book is incredible and if I could add anything I would add nothing to the book except this review.

~ MARK G.

When I was told about The Ghostly Adventures of Jamie C. O'Hare, I was amazed. The book is so extravagant, and I think that Jamie is a very adventurous boy, seeking out trouble! Exuberant as the book is, it is unfathomably exciting, filled with plot-twists and suspense! What a wonderful book to read, as well as a book filled with passion and depth! 5 stars!

~ LIAM S.

CHAPTER ONE

For a kid, boredom sometimes feels like a fate worse than death. But for me, it took that year to realize that boredom can be a welcome relief. I certainly hadn't figured that out during the long drive to Black Creek, much of it through forested areas and up and down rolling hills with almost no cell phone reception. Five hours felt like an eternity in the backseat with only a few games on my phone until the outskirts of my new hometown finally appeared in the headlights of our minivan.

I had practically begged Mom to download new games before the drive. She insisted I had enough to play and she wasn't paying for more. I liked those Apps when I was ten, but I'd mastered all of their levels a long time ago. There's a big difference between ten and twelve and Mom just didn't seem to get that. Truthfully, I went through video games pretty fast and was in constant need of updates or new ones. Read a book, Mom said, but I knew that would put me to sleep, and sleep was something I needed to avoid unless I couldn't help it.

Janine had given up on her phone just after midnight and was snoring in the passenger seat, ending her nonstop complaining that her life was over. Apparently, a few hours without texting her friends was situation critical. Pressing record, I slipped my phone onto the console between Mom and Janine. I was glad Janine was sleeping but not just for the blackmail material to use against her. I wanted to see Black Creek myself for the first time without having to listen to my sister trash the place. She'd been doing that ever since Mom announced the move, even though she'd never seen our new house or any part of the village except in pictures.

The village was in the middle of nowhere. My phone showed that it had full reception once we drove past the Welcome to Black Creek sign, Population 1226. Before that, I was lucky to get one bar. The sign was a standard green road sign with reflective lettering. Nothing special. Just like the village, or so I thought.

The downtown, if you could call it that, was visible in the distance. Even in the hazy darkness, I could tell the place was tiny, nothing like Newbury. A church dominated the skyline. As it got closer, I wiped away the fog on my back window, smearing droplets against the glass. I pushed the button and the familiar hum let in the warm late summer air. I inhaled deeply. A light popped on in the tower window of the approaching church, interrupting the quiet desertion of the street.

Who could be up there this late at night?

And then a soft whisper called my name.

"Jaaammmmiiieeeeee...."

I spun around and peered out the back window at the church diminishing behind us. The building was in darkness.

"That's weird," I said.

"What's weird?" Mom asked, her eyes fixed on the road.

"A light went on in the church tower, and I thought I heard something."

"Are you sure? I didn't hear anything, and I would have noticed a light go on," Mom said.

"Forget it," I yawned. "I'm tired. It's probably nothing.

CHAPTER TWO

I bounded up the stairs to see my new bedroom. Lucky for us, Mom had told the movers where to put our furniture and paid them to put our beds together. I was tired after the long drive and couldn't imagine helping Mom assemble my bed, not to mention the complaining that would come from Janine. Smart move, Mom.

I looked around, evaluating the layout. My furniture had been perfect for my old bedroom, compact and organized. Mom was obsessed with decorating for small spaces like our old apartment, and she had tons of books and magazines on the subject. But here, in this larger room, my single bed, night stand, desk, and dresser just looked funny.

And what was with the wallpaper? Orange, green, and brown happy faces stared at me from all angles of the room. It was kind of disturbing.

When Mom showed us the photos of the house, Janine and I had both wanted the bedroom with a view of the backyard and no happy face wallpaper. She got it, of course. She always got her way. It didn't matter what I wanted or what my reasons were. Mom just gave in to Janine so she wouldn't have to argue with her for hours. I wondered if Mom realized she was creating a teenage monster!

"What are you doing, puke-face? Isn't it way past your bedtime?" Janine asked.

I'm sure my sister just wanted to check out my new room, but as usual, she couldn't resist an opportunity to harass me.

"You are still a baby after all," she chided.

Mom appeared in my doorway, struggling with a tall stack of bed linens. I rushed to help her, relieving her of my comforter and pillow.

"Thank you, Jamie. Janine, you can make your bed. Your linens are in your room."

"Fine, Marion. Good night, wittle brodder."

"Get lost, Janine!"

"Stop! Both of you!" Mom scolded. " It's been a long day. Let's get to bed."

It was times like that where I thought I hated my sister.

Yes, I knew I should try to get along with her, but she was fifteen and didn't make it easy. We were so different that if you didn't know any better, you'd never believe we were related. Janine was tall, blond, and skinny. I was short with a stubborn layer of baby fat and thick light brown hair. She had brown eyes, and I had blue eyes. She was a "mean girl," and popular at school, while I was quiet and shy. We were complete opposites. I didn't think we'd ever get along.

After Janine left, Mom and I smoothed out my sheets and comforter.

"Good night, Jamie," Mom said. "I like your bedroom.

Don't worry about that wallpaper. We'll get rid of it soon."

"Thanks Mom."

She gave me a quick peck on my forehead and walked out.

I threw my pajamas on and jumped into bed. I hoped I wouldn't have another weird dream or worse, a nightmare. I had so many in Newbury that had left me clutching the sheets in the middle of the night. Maybe Black Creek would be different. The nightmares seemed so clear at the time, but left me with only fragments in my memory when I woke up. I'd try to forget until the flashbacks started that interrupted my thoughts, stubbornly making their presence known. With no order or sense to any of it, I hoped that being a normal kid wasn't a thing of the past.

Luckily, my head barely hit the pillow before I fell into a deep sleep.

It was one of those times where I just couldn't help it.

Chapter Three

Desperately, I fumbled through the papers scattered on the desk.

Where were the keys? Where? Pens, pencils, and papers fell to the floor. I kept hunting.

Seconds felt like hours.

Finally! There they were, sitting underneath a church bulletin.

I sat in the desk chair, my hands shaking, and fumbled to insert one of the small keys into the keyhole of the bottom drawer of the desk. It didn't fit.

I tried another one. The lock clicked, releasing. I quickly but carefully pulled the drawer open.

Bang, Bang, Bang!

The door shook from the force of an angry fist.

I looked up. Shadows danced through the crack between the door and floor.

"Open up! We know you're in there!"

I pulled the folded paper from my pocket, shoved it deep into the desk drawer, locked it and pulled the handle, just to be sure. It didn't budge.

They didn't find it the first time, and there was no way I was going to let them find it this time! Now to hide the keys.

The tiny room had only the small wooden desk, the one chair, and a stack of cardboard boxes against the back wall. Not many choices.

Bang, Bang, Bang!

I was running out of time.

"Get something to pick this lock!" the voice barked at someone.

Heavy footsteps thumped down the stairs.

No time! Where, where, where?

Bang, Bang, Bang!

My heart pounded in my ears. I had to decide!

I rushed to the boxes, removed the first two from the stack and opened the third. I shifted the contents around, shoved the keys right to the bottom, closed the flaps and stacked the other two boxes on top.

The door burst open.

A sharp pain radiated through my chest. I took a deep breath, but nothing entered my lungs.

"Where is it?" the kid asked.

I fell to my knees. Everything went black.

CHAPTER FOUR

"Jamie, wake up!"

My eyes snapped open. I looked around the room, bleary-eyed and a little shaken from the dream.

"You've been sleeping forever!" Janine cried. "It's after ten. Are you going to laze around all day?"

"Get out of my room, Janine." I was not in the mood to deal with her.

Instead of leaving, she plopped herself down at the end of my single bed.

"I'm not going anywhere, fart-breath."

Janine had a broad vocabulary of gross names for me, usually involving disgusting bodily functions or conditions.

"Other than Mom, you're the only one I know in this hick town, so you're stuck with me for now," she complained. "What's there to do in this boring village, anyway?"

I sat up on the bed. "If I knew that, I'd be doing it and not talking to you."

“I meant for teenagers like me, not toddlers like you.”

“Get out, Janine!”

“Fine! I don’t want to be around a stinky fungus, anyway!”

As she stood up, she whipped her head around and her long blond hair hit me in the face before she walked out the door.

I reluctantly rolled out of bed, grabbed a pair of grey cargo shorts and a blue t-shirt from one of my boxes and put them on. That crazy dream flashed back through my mind - the frantic search, the pounding on the door, the pain in my chest. Where was that room? And what was I trying to hide?

A familiar sensation washed over me. This was no ordinary dream.

I tried to distract myself and unpacked a few of my boxes, stacking my hoodies on a shelf in the closet.

I hung my mirror over my dresser and straightened the stubborn clump of hair that was sticking up on the side of my head. And like always, it popped right back up again. I gave up and instead placed my laptop and mystery novels neatly on my desk. I set the framed photo of my dad on my night stand and I pinned my “Military Masters” poster above my bed.

Now my room was feeling more like home.

I grabbed the empty boxes, went downstairs, and stacked them in the foyer.

“Going out for a bit, Mom.”

It was time to check out my new neighborhood.

CHAPTER FIVE

I plopped down on our porch steps and looked around, the sun warming my legs.

Across the street, a short, round, middle-aged man was mowing the lawn of a blue bungalow. He looked up and waved at me. I waved too, and he smiled and went back to working. He seemed friendly. Hopefully, the kids in the neighborhood were too. I wasn't looking forward to being the new kid in town. Not on top of everything else.

My Dad died the summer before and after that my life changed—big time! Sure, I was sad, and I missed my Dad a lot, but that's when I started seeing and hearing strange things. It was as if Dad's death flipped a switch in my brain and turned something on, something I couldn't explain. I started having nightmares and images would pop into my head, a face or a building I didn't recognize, and then they'd disappear. Other times, I heard whispers, like the one I heard on our drive into the village. Someone would talk to me, but I couldn't make out all the words. It was all pretty scary.

I thought about telling Janine. She also lost Dad, so maybe she'd understand and not be mean for once. But I figured she'd just laugh at me and call me a baby. I tried talking to Mom about it. She said it was just nightmares because of my grief over Dad's death.

Mom did eventually become worried when I started yelling in my sleep every other night. As if that weren't enough, Janine developed a seriously bad attitude. She started calling Mom by her first name and was constantly fighting with her and staying out past her curfew. Hardly a day passed without Janine storming to her room and slamming the door. Plus, Mom needed to find a better job to pay the medical bills from Dad's long hospital stays.

All of this led to Mom deciding we should move. She said a change would be good for all of us. By the end of June, she'd found work as a real estate agent here in Black Creek and the rest is history.

I reached down and grabbed some pebbles beside the porch steps and threw them one by one at an imaginary target on the grass. Black Creek seemed boring compared to what I was used to, the constant hustle and bustle of the city and cool stuff to do steps away from our apartment building. At least if we'd moved in September, I could have gone to school. It would have been something to do, even if I was the new kid. But no, Mom had to start her job before then, and the new house was ours at the end of July. So, it was only the beginning of August and here we were. I had the rest of the summer to kill.

In between throws, I kept scanning my new street. An old woman was weeding the giant garden of her grey stone house to my left. She looked up, frowned at me, and went right back to pulling.

"I guess not everyone is friendly."

A fat black cat emerged from the shade of the large maple tree on our lawn. After a long and lazy stretch, it sauntered up the driveway toward the house on my right. Like mine, the house had two stories and white siding, but its front door was a bright red instead of black, like ours.

As the cat climbed the porch steps, a girl in a striped yellow T-shirt and blue shorts came out of the front door and sat down on a wicker rocking chair. She looked about my age with long black hair and olive skin. The fat cat flicked its tail and plopped itself down at her feet.

The girl had just put in earbuds when she noticed me. Right away, she stood up, put her phone and earbuds in her pocket, and called out.

"Hey!"

She walked toward me with a big smile, with the fat cat following close behind. I stood up to greet her.

"Hi," I murmured.

"You're the new kid," she said, tucking her thick hair behind her ears. She was thinner and shorter than me and had bright blue eyes. And she was cute. My face flushed.

"Yes, that's me," I said, a little louder that time.

I shifted my feet and stared at the ground.

The girl broke the awkward silence. "I'm Maggie Zhou, and you are?"

I quickly came to my senses. I felt like such a dork.

"Oh, sorry! I'm Jamie O'Hare."

"I saw the trucks leave yesterday. Are you all done moving in?"

"Yep. We're still unpacking though."

The cat was rubbing itself against my legs. I reached down and gave its ears a good scratch.

"That's my cat, Marjorie," Maggie said. "She's pretty spoiled, and it shows! Has anyone shown you around Black Creek yet?"

"Not yet. We drove in late last night and it was dark. Is there much to do around here?"

"Of course, there is! I'll take you on a tour."

"OK. I'll tell my mom," I said and rushed back into the house.

CHAPTER SIX

I rejoined Maggie on the front porch, ready for her guided tour of Black Creek. Mom had tried to convince Janine and I that we'd make friends easily when she gave us the news about the move. Maybe she was right.

"I know the change will be hard for you, but Black Creek is full of kids," she assured us. "This move will be good for both of you and for me. With my new job, I can afford to buy us our own house. We can all push restart. You'll grow to love it!"

"I can't believe you're doing this to me, Marian." Janine whined and then predictably stormed out of the apartment.

I, on the other hand, asked a lot of questions.

"Are there kids my age around? Where will I go to school? What is there to do there?"

I googled Black Creek, but the village didn't have much of a website. There were a few pictures of the park, some stores, and a few local baseball teams, but that was it.

As we walked down our street, Maggie did all the talking. She was an only child, she told me. Her family moved to

Black Creek when she was five, and now she was twelve. She loved to read, she played soccer and took guitar lessons. Her favorite foods were peanut butter on toast for breakfast, and salt-and-vinegar chips for a snack. She broke her arm a few months before when she fell out of the tree in her backyard.

"I like to sit in my tree when I need some time to myself," she explained. "That day I picked a branch too high up and it broke."

Maggie talked a lot, but that was okay with me. I didn't feel like talking anyway, at least not about myself.

The end of our street intersected with Black Creek Road, the main street which divided the village between the north and the south.

"Let's go this way," Maggie said, and we turned right, walking down Black Creek Road. "It'll take us to the shops."

Black Creek looked like a typical village, the kind I'd seen in movies and on TV. Old-fashioned looking street lamps, trees, and large potted plants lined the sidewalks. There was a Community Centre, a coffee shop called the Daily Ground and a General Store called Mervin's in the middle of the village.

Maggie told me about a song she was learning to play on the guitar, and how she had to keep practicing for an upcoming recital as we passed the General Store and reached the coffee shop. A few people were having lunch on the patio.

"They have great lattes here," Maggie said. "I can only have decaf because Mom says that I don't need the extra energy. Right now, they have cotton-candy flavored lattes for kids. They're my favorite, but you can only get them in the summer."

"Do you hang out here?" I asked. "I used to go to places like this with my friends in Newbury."

"My friend Angus and I come here sometimes, or we go to the park."

I knew from my online research that the park in the center of the village was next to the church I had seen with the spooky light. It was named after a local war hero, Mitchell Green. The few pictures that were on the website showed big old maple and willow trees surrounding a baseball diamond, a basketball court, a playground, and a large picnic area.

Maggie continued. "Sometimes there's stuff going on at the Community Centre, and we'll hang out there. You'll like Angus. He's really cool."

A girl who looked about our age was putting a poster up on the front door of the Daily Ground.

Maggie greeted her. "Hey, Sydney."

The girl finished smoothing the paper over the glass and turned to us. She had spiky blond hair and wore a fluorescent green headband, a tie-dyed T-shirt, and faded blue jeans. She had black and brown leather bracelets on both arms.

"Hi Maggie." She nodded at me and walked away.

"Is that a friend of yours, Maggie?"

"I know her but we're not close. Her name is Sydney Raymond. She goes to my school. She's in my class, but we don't hang out."

"What does the poster say?" I asked, walking over to the coffee shop door. Maggie followed.

"That looks like fun," I said. "Something to do before school starts."

"It should be! Everyone's talking about it. Sydney's uncle is Father Joe, the priest at the church. She must be putting the posters up to help him out. I wonder if she'll go."

"Why wouldn't she go?" I asked.

"Sydney's… just different from most kids. None of the kids at school know her very well. I think it's because she keeps to herself," Maggie said. "As for the Anniversary Celebration, she's interested in Black Creek history, but the church stuff just doesn't seem like her thing. She started a blog called the *SydyBlog*, which has over 300 followers. The posts and articles on it are about UFOs, conspiracy theories, and local hauntings. She believes the first moon landing was faked and filmed in Hollywood, and she posts a bunch of articles and videos about that. Angus thinks she's a genius."

"She sounds pretty cool," I said.

What did Maggie mean by local hauntings? After what I saw and heard at the church on the way into the village, I would have to check out Sydney's blog.

Chapter Seven

Maggie and I continued down Black Creek Road, passing several multi-story brick buildings with shops on the ground floors and apartments and businesses on the upper floors. I noticed Sydney's posters on many of the shop doors and lamp posts.

Maggie pointed to the buildings and landmarks across the street.

"And that's the library." She motioned to a small stone building with a big green wooden door. "I go there sometimes to do homework, but not very often. I'm not a good student. It drives my parents crazy!"

Maggie turned to look at me. "I've only been talking about me. My mom tells me I need to let other people talk. What's your story, Jamie? Why did you move here?"

"Uh, it's fine. I don't mind hearing about you."

"No." Maggie shook her head. "Tell me. I'd like to know."

"Well, okay." We started walking again as I talked. "I moved here yesterday, which you know, from Newbury with my mom and my older sister Janine. She's fifteen."

I knew I had to get it over with, so I added, "My dad died last year, and my mom got a new job as a real estate agent here in Black Creek."

"Sorry about your dad. That must be hard."

"Thanks. It is sometimes."

I tried my best to hold back tears, something I'd gotten used to doing that year, but this time, I just couldn't. They pooled in my eyelids, ready to spill over at any moment. I looked at the ground and wiped my eyes with the back of my hand, hoping Maggie didn't notice. If she did, she said nothing.

"What about your friends from Newbury?" she asked. "Do you think you'll see them again?"

"Maybe. I don't know."

Please don't ask me more about that, Maggie, I silently begged. I didn't know if I still had friends back home. Things didn't exactly end well before we moved. After my visions and nightmares started, I worked up the nerve to talk about it with my friend Sanjay one afternoon. I started out by asking him if he believed in ghosts. It was close to Halloween, so it wasn't an odd question.

"Um ... no, not really, Jamie. I like scary movies and video games with ghosts and zombies and stuff, but it's not real!"

I dropped it after that. I thought Sanjay or my other friends would make fun of me. I started missing school when the nightmares kept me up at night. I had black circles under my eyes and was tired all of the time. I stopped texting my friends and eventually, they stopped texting and trying to get together. I didn't blame them. I wasn't much fun anymore.

Up ahead, I could see the grey stone church, with its many stained-glass windows and its tall wide steeple. A stone statue of an angel stood in the center of a graveyard beside the church overlooking its occupants. Manicured lawn and blooming gardens surrounded the crooked old white tombstones. A small red brick bungalow sat beside the church, presumably the priest's house, where Sydney's uncle lived.

I was eager to change the subject so, I pointed and said the first thing I that came into my mind.

"Hey, is that the church?"

"Of course, it is. What did you think it was?"

Okay, so it was a pretty dumb thing to ask.

"I guess it's pretty obvious it's a church!" I muttered.

"Hey, sorry if I was rude," Maggie said as she rubbed her arms and shivered.

"That's okay. "What's wrong?

"That church gives me the chills."

"Why?" I asked, remembering that strange light and the voice. Maybe the same thing had happened to Maggie.

She shrugged. "I have no idea. There's just something creepy about it. It gives me goosebumps. Maybe it's the graveyard. Graveyards are always spooky! They remind me of that old zombie movie, the one where the dead crawl out of graves and you can see hands reach out from the ground."

"I haven't seen that one, but it sounds scary!"

"I've seen way too many horror movies! They're my favorite type of movie. If you want to hang out with me, get ready for a few scary TV nights," Maggie warned.

As we were passing the church, she began telling me about her favorite shows. I was smiling. I couldn't wait to join Maggie in one of her movie nights. But then—

“Jaaammiiieeee…Jaaaaammmiiiieeeee…”a voice whispered.

Startled, I looked at Maggie.

“Did you hear that?”

Was I hearing things again?

Was someone staring at us? I was certain that we were being watched. I looked around and canvassed the area for prying eyes.

Ice cold shivers crept down my spine.

“Hear what?” Maggie asked.

“Jaaammiiieeee… Jaaaaaammmmmiiiieeeee…” the voice whispered again.

I swallowed hard. Should I tell Maggie? She thought the church was creepy, so she might believe me. But no. Maggie would think there’s something wrong with me if I started telling her about that. I didn’t want to lose a friend right after meeting her.

“Jamie?” Maggie followed up after I didn’t answer.

We picked up our pace, and the church was behind us.

“It was probably just the wind,” I said trying to convince myself more than Maggie.

“I didn’t hear anything, but as usual, creep factor of 9 out of 10 from that place!” Maggie said.

I looked back at the church and shivered.

“Yeah, creep factor for sure.”

CHAPTER EIGHT

"Let's visit Angus," Maggie suggested. "He lives on the north side of the village, and he has a pool! We've been using it a lot this summer, and I bet he'll ask you to join us!"

It was getting hot, and that pool sounded fantastic. Angus lived in the little neighborhood south-east of the main street. It wasn't very far away, but the midday sun was beating down on us as we crossed the park.

We approached a grey bungalow with white shutters and a bright orange front door. Bikes, balls, and hockey sticks littered the front yard. A basketball net hung over the door of the attached garage.

"That's Angus' house. He has three brothers and a cute bulldog named Roofus."

Just then, two young boys with bright red curly hair ran out the front door and grabbed their bikes, Roofus barking behind them. The boys looked exactly the same! They were even wearing matching grey striped shorts and black t-shirts.

"Hi, Maggie! Bye, Maggie!" they said as they rode away.

"See you, Callum. Bye, Mikey. As you can tell, Angus's younger brothers are identical twins. They like to dress the same to mess with people."

Four kids, parents, and a dog. How did they all fit in that small house?

I followed Maggie to the front door. She rang the doorbell and a tall, thin woman with shoulder-length red hair opened the door.

"Well, hello Maggie!" she said warmly. "Always nice to see you. And whom do we have here?"

The woman smiled, looking me up and down.

"This is Jamie O'Hare, Mrs. Fisher. He's new to Black Creek. His family just moved in today."

"It's nice to meet you, Jamie. Welcome to our tiny village. I'm sure you'll love it here! I'd like to meet your mom soon."

"Thanks, Mrs. Fisher. I'll tell her. Nice to meet you too."

"Angus is in his room with his face in front of his computer as usual! Maybe you can convince him to clean his room, Jamie." Mrs. Fisher chuckled.

Maggie led the way down the hallway to Angus' room, the last doorway on the left.

"Hey, Angus," Maggie said.

Angus was sitting at his desk with his back to us, watching a video on his computer. His room was a mess! There were clothes piled all over his bed, and video games were scattered around his desk chair on the dark wood floor. The smell of dirty laundry filled the air.

How could anyone hang out in this room? I thought.

"Hey, Maggie." Angus greeted her without turning around. "I think I've figured out how to beat Military Masters! This online video is explaining the last level."

"You've been working on that for what, five minutes? Angus is a computer whiz," Maggie explained. "He figures out video games by decoding them, and he creates his own Apps."

"That's amazing! Military Masters is my favorite game!" I said excitedly.

Maggie sat down on the bed and pushed Angus' clothes aside so I could sit beside her on the green and dark blue plaid comforter.

"Don't be too impressed. Angus is good at gaming, but none of his Apps actually work."

"Way to burst my bubble, Maggie! One day, I'm going to sell one of my Apps and get rich! I'll be able to buy all the computer equipment I want."

"By the way, Angus, this is Jamie O'Hare. He's the new kid that moved in next door to me."

"Hey, Jamie."

Angus turned his desk chair around to look at me. He had green eyes and square, black-rimmed glasses. His chin length strawberry blond hair lay flat against his face. I noticed that his long, skinny legs stuck out well past the end of his seat.

I was pretty sure he'd tower over me if he stood up!

"Did you guys bring me snacks?" Angus asked.

"No! Sometimes I bring Angus extra homemade stuff that my mom makes," Maggie explained."He eats pretty much non-stop."

"Well, yeah," Angus replied with a shrug. "My mom says that I'm in a growth spurt."

Maggie laughed. "A never-ending one!"

Angus asked me about Military Masters and other video games he liked to play. We compared phones and talked about some new Apps we wanted to download.

"I want to code video games when I grow up," he said.

"That would be so much fun!" I said. I shifted closer to Angus' chair and bent over to look at some of his games on the floor.

"I want to be a character in one of your games, especially if it's a zombie or ghost hunter game," Maggie said.

"I'll make you my sidekick," Angus said.

Maggie frowned. "I want to be the leader!"

"We'll see."

Angus was pretty awesome, stinky room or not.

I thought it would be so hard to make friends here and that Black Creek would be boring, but I'd already made two, and it was only my first day!

Other than that strange whispering at the church, things were going better than okay.

And Maggie and Angus both seemed interested in the paranormal. Maybe one day, after we got to know each other a little more, I could tell them about what was going on with me.

One day. Maybe soon. But not yet.

CHAPTER NINE

Knock... Knock... Knock ...

The sound from the glass jarred me from my sleep.

Knock... Knock... Knock ...

What was that? I glanced at the window. My curtains were closed.

I'd been in Black Creek for two weeks, hanging out with Maggie and Angus almost every day. We'd text one another after breakfast and meet up. We'd go to the coffee shop, watch movies, play video games, ride our bikes, walk Roofus, or go swimming at Angus's house. Black Creek was feeling more and more like home, even better than my old home. I was having so much fun and no bad dreams, voices or visions. I thought the move was the restart that Mom predicted.

But now, this.

It's only the branches on the tree outside, I told myself. I turned over in bed, my back to the window. I just needed to fall asleep and ignore the noise.

Only I couldn't, not with the wind whistling outside and heavy rain pelting the house.

Knock! Knock! Knock!

Again! Three steady raps against the glass.

I forced myself out of bed and took slow, deliberate steps toward the window. Maybe the noise will stop before I get there.

Knock! Knock! Knock!

Louder that time.

Knock, knock! Knock, knock, knock!

More desperate that time.

I grabbed the curtains and slowly pulled them open.

An old man was staring in at me!

Paralyzed by fear, I tried to move, tried to look away, but couldn't. Deep wrinkles lined his pale, pasty skin. He was bald on top with thick grey hair on the sides of his head above his ears, and a wispy grey beard. His face was expressionless. He stared at me intensely out of empty black eyes.

My blood ran cold.

There was only a pane of glass between us!

I focused all my energy on breaking the terrifying grip of the old man's stare. I still couldn't move. Somehow, I managed to force my eyes closed.

Three deep breaths. "One. Two. Three."

I opened my eyes. Nothing there, just the rain running down my window and the dark night sky. I looked down at the street below.

Nobody was out there. No ladder or other evidence of how the old man got up to my window. I pulled on the curtains to close them in case he came back but one of the curtain hooks caught on the rod. I forgot the curtains, jumped into bed and buried my face in my pillow.

Not real, not real, not real, I told myself over and over when....

Bang, bang, bang!

I screamed.

Moments later, Mom ran into my room.

"Are you okay, Jamie?"

I kept my head under the covers.

"Jamie, it's just your old window. The latch is unlocked," Mom said, her voice calm.

I turned to watch as she grabbed each window pane, lined them up side by side and secured the lock, the wind tossing her auburn hair. She shook the window, making sure the lock was snug.

"I know. I'm sorry, Mom. I'm fine."

I was trembling under my blankets but tried not to show it. I didn't want her to worry anymore. She had worried enough when we lived in Newbury.

"I'll get you a glass of water," she said and disappeared down the stairs.

Just then Janine appeared in my doorway. I guess the commotion had woken her up. I should have felt bad about that, but I didn't.

"Aw, did the wittle baby have a nightmare?"

"Go away, Janine!" I said, throwing my pillow at her.

"You're such a freak!" She leaned against the door frame and grinned at me. "You really should see a shrink."

"It's none of your business!"

"Whatever. I can't believe you woke me up! I'm going back to bed."

"That's a great idea, Janine," Mom said, walking back into the room.

Janine turned and flounced away as Mom retrieved the pillow.

"Here you go, Jamie."

Mom placed the glass of water on my night stand and fluffed my pillow.

"I know that work is taking a lot of my time and I'm not around as much as I used to be, but you can talk to me if your nightmares are still happening."

"I know, Mom." I didn't want to say anything more.

"Okay then. Good night. See you in the morning." She kissed me on the forehead and walked out of the room.

"Night, Mom." But I knew I wouldn't fall asleep for a long time. I was too upset. It was happening again! The whispering and now the visions were back. And I thought maybe, just maybe, I'd left it all behind.

CHAPTER TEN

I woke up late the next morning after finally falling into a restless sleep. I lay in bed trying to figure out why my life had turned into such a freak show.

No wonder I hadn't told my friends. It made no sense to me. I couldn't imagine telling Maggie and Angus.

The only person I'd ever talked to about my nightmares and visions was Grandma. After months of suffering in silence, I decided to confess everything when she was visiting us in Newbury last Christmas. As a retired judge, she was a good listener. She always made me feel like I could tell her anything that was on my mind, so if anyone would understand, she would.

"Jamie, dear," Grandma said in her most comforting tone. "What you have is a 'special sight' just like your Grandpa Cornelius. You must have inherited it from him because your Dad never had to deal with it. Your Grandpa said some people call it a 'gift,' but that makes it sound like something given to you because you want it or need it. He didn't see it that way. He called it 'special,' because it's rare or different, and a 'sight,' because it let him see certain things. In his case and now yours, it's the ability to see things others can't."

Normally, I tuned out when Grandma talked about Grandpa Cornelius. It's not like I didn't care to hear about him. I had his name as my middle name, so I couldn't help but feel a connection. But I'd never met him and Grandma talked about him all the time, even telling me about the boring stuff like the lunches he used to pack for work.

But this Grandpa Cornelius story was worth listening to.

"Will it go away?" I asked.

"I can't predict that for you," Grandma said. "Your grandpa had it for his entire life. It bothered him when he was young, but less so as he got older. Maybe it's bothering you because you're just not ready for it yet, not ready to see and hear what's being put in front of you. So, until then, if these visions and sounds happen and you're scared, close your eyes and take three deep breaths. That's what your Grandpa did when he was your age. It will pass like a cool breeze on a hot day. Just remember that one day, you may decide you're ready for it. And when you do, maybe you can use your special sight to help people."

I thanked Grandma, and I followed her advice. So, when the whispers and images came, I'd close my eyes and count my breaths. One. Two. Three. Just like I'd done when I saw the old man in my bedroom window.

It made it easier to get through them, but it didn't make it stop. The nightmares were keeping me awake, and that was when my visions had been quick flashes of images. Last night was different. I saw that old man so clearly. He had looked so real and that had never happened before.

Why couldn't I just be normal like other kids?

Eventually I rolled out of bed, got dressed, and made my way downstairs. I grabbed a blueberry muffin from the kitchen island and took a giant bite.

It looked like Mom had already left for work. Janine was up watching something on her phone in the family room, just off the kitchen.

She looked up from her phone and glared at me. "You were yelling in your sleep last night. Good thing it stopped after I left your room. Try not to keep me awake anymore. I get these horrible bags under my eyes."

Why couldn't she be nice to me, even for a minute? I ignored her.

"Are your nightmares starting again?" she asked.

Janine actually sounded somewhat concerned. I didn't buy the act. She had no sympathy for me back in Newbury when I was screaming myself awake and was up half of the night. Why would she be any different now?

"None of your business," I said. I took another muffin and sat at the opposite end of the couch.

The doorbell rang just as I was taking another bite.

"I'll get it." Janine stood up. As she left the family room, she looked over her shoulder and said, "You're welcome!"

I rolled my eyes.

"He's in the family room. I'll leave you two for your play date," Janine said from the foyer as Maggie walked into the room. "I'm going to hang out at the park with Brittany and Kendra. Where are you guys going?"

"Yet again, none of your business," I replied.

And I didn't care where Janine planned to go with her

friends. She had wasted no time in finding followers since we moved to Black Creek.

"I'm supposed to know where you are. Marian's orders," Janine called. "Trust me! I'm not happy about keeping track of you infants."

"We're going to Angus' house," Maggie interjected.

"Lock the door when you go out. Bye, Cornelius."

The front door slammed.

"Is she always like that?" Maggie asked.

"Yep. Pretty much."

"Sometimes I'm happy I don't have any sisters or brothers! By the way, who's Cornelius?"

My face flushed. "Um, that's my middle name."

"Cool!" Maggie said.

Yet another reason Maggie was turning out to be such a great friend!

"We should get going," said Maggie. "Angus texted me last night and wants to show us the new App he built and then go for a swim after."

"Sounds good!" I said.

I ran upstairs to get my swim trunks and then we headed out the door into the late morning air.

Chapter Eleven

"Did Angus tell you anything about his App?" I asked Maggie as we walked.

"He said he wants to surprise us. I know he's been working on a few different ones. One of them is a bad breath reader, so if he holds his phone up to our mouths when we get there, we'll know it's that one!"

I laughed.

We usually took the longer route and walked through the village. Mervin's changed their front window twice every week, so we liked to check it out. Sometimes, we bought iced lattes at the Daily Ground for the walk.

But every time Maggie and I approached the church over the last few weeks, that same chill went down my spine. I'd feel those eyes staring at me, boring into the back of my head. It would be nice to avoid that. Plus, I was still jumpy from my vision of that old man.

"Hey, let's cut through the park today," I said.

"Sure. That's fine with me. Like I told you that church

creeps me out, anyway."

"Me too. I feel like we're being watched whenever we walk by. Weird that we both think it's creepy."

I left it at that for now, but maybe one day soon, I could tell Maggie more.

Angus was in his driveway shooting hoops when we arrived. I grabbed the extra basketball and took a shot. It hit the backboard and bounced in.

I threw my arms in the air and cheered, "Yes!"

I wasn't particularly athletic, but I did like to play basketball.

Angus and Maggie were fighting for a ball when Angus's brother, Donny, and Donny's friends, Rodney Bucci and Ricky Tyler, walked out of the house.

"Great shot!" Rodney said. His voice dripped with sarcasm and he started slow clapping. "Look! The nerd patrol can play a sport!"

Rodney was short and stocky with light blond curly hair, a thick neck, and a permanent scowl on his face. He wore cut-off camo cargo pants and a black t-shirt with "I'm the Real Deal" in white lettering. His high-top running shoes had no laces, so the tongues of his shoes flopped over.

Rodney's voice became nastier. "Get lost," he said. "We're playing now! Go and find some more nerds to play with."

One of the guy's arms was the size of three of mine combined. There was no way Maggie, Angus, and I would win a fight for the court with him.

We'd had a few run ins with Rodney in town and in the park since I moved to Black Creek. He always made fun of us, calling us nerds, and taking over the pool at Angus's house. Donny and Ricky followed him around like puppies. This morning was no different. The two of them just stood there staring at us, saying nothing.

Angus looked over at Maggie and me. "Let's go the coffee shop," he said.

"I knew you nerds were smart!" Rodney said.

Angus and I surrendered the basketballs, and Rodney, Donny, and Ricky immediately played.

We walked away, but Maggie's face flushed with anger.

"Why are we leaving? We can't keep letting them get their way! Those guys are such jerks! Angus, can't you do something about your brother and his stupid friends?"

I didn't blame Maggie for being upset. Those guys got under my skin too.

Angus shrugged. "I've tried, but there's no point. I tell my mom, and she talks to Donny but they wait until my mom isn't around to act like that. When I complain to my mom, Donny just denies it and then picks on me even worse. There's no point. Let's just go."

Angus changed the subject. "Hey, I can't wait to show you my new App!"

"I can't wait to see it!" I said.

Maggie was ahead of us and said nothing during the trip through the park. She was obviously still mad at Angus's brother and his friends—or at us for giving in so easily.

We caught up with her as we reached Black Creek Road, and we crossed the street to the Daily Ground together.

Maggie and I ordered three cotton candy iced lattes, while Angus grabbed the table in the corner by the front window. We returned with the drinks and Angus took a quick sip of his latte before describing his App.

"I'm super excited! This is the coolest App I've ever built! Maggie, remember when we watched those paranormal investigation video a few months ago?"

"No, not the details. We used to watch those videos a lot before we switched to old horror movies."

"You know, the one where I complained because they tried to record ghosts in dark rooms so you can never see anything," Angus said. "That's when I told you I could build better ghost detection tools than the ones they use in the show."

"Oh, yes," Maggie said. "And I told you I didn't know why you'd want to."

My interest in this App was growing by the minute.

"And then I said I like a challenge!" Angus said. "Well, I've been working on an App ever since. I programmed software to read electro-magnetic energy. It measures the amount of energy and pinpoints its location. You can use the App on your smart phone with the camera. You open the App and just point your phone and look around to see where the energy is. The energy looks pink, on screen. I also bought a mini antenna that you insert into the phone. I adapted it to detect electro-magnetic energy measurable when it mixes with oxygen in the air. The App reads it, and the phone beeps."

"Speak English please, Angus," Maggie demanded.

"The antenna detects paranormal energy, and the App reads it," I said. "And you can see it on the screen of your phone."

"Now that's better! Thank you, Jamie," Maggie said. "But Angus, where do you think you'll ever use something like that?"

"You never know when it could come in handy! It doesn't hurt to be prepared. Maybe I'll sell it to one of those famous paranormal investigators!"

"We'll see about that," Maggie said. She took a sip of her latte.

"I think it's cool!" I said. "Show us how it works."

I was thinking I should have that App open in my room at night! It could warn me before I had another scary vision or dream.

"Be careful, Angus! Remember the mood reader App you built?" Maggie turned to me. "Angus thought he could build an App to read your mood, and it would show as a certain color on your phone. Like, if you're mad, the screen would turn bright red. If you're happy or excited, the screen would turn purple. And if you're sad, it would turn blue. Instead, it fried Angus' phone when he tried it out. He had to do chores for a month to get a new one!"

Angus grinned. "Hey! I still believe in that technology. Anyway, it's time to test my latest creation!"

He put his phone on the table, inserted the antenna and held it up, scanning the area. A couple sitting at a nearby table looked up curiously and then went back to their conversation.

"It didn't fry my phone! Victory is mine!" Angus cheered.

"But keep listening. If the App detects any paranormal energy, it'll beep fast and loudly."

He reached across the table and scanned the area around Maggie's head with his phone.

"Maybe you're possessed, Maggie!" I said.

Maggie laughed and held her hand up to wave the phone away.

"The only thing that App is going to detect is the stench of your smelly feet, Angus!"

"Now, you, Jamie," Angus said, waving his phone around my arm and then around my head.

"I'm not so sure about this!" I thought.

BAH! BAH! BAH! BAH!!!

Chapter Twelve

The three of us nearly jumped off our chairs!

"I don't think that's my App," Angus said. "The screen looks normal."

"Was that the alarm on your phone?" Maggie asked me. "I'm practically wearing my latte! What did you set your alarm for?"

"I didn't set the alarm." I pulled my phone out of my pocket and double checked. "It must be acting funny."

Angus frowned. "Darn it! At first, I thought it might be my App."

I opened the settings on my phone and noticed that the alarm was off. I showed Maggie and Angus.

"Strange," Maggie said.

"Yeah, that's weird. Do you want me to look at it?" Angus offered.

"Maybe. But let's give it a few days and see if the alarm goes off again by itself."

"Okay. Let me know," Angus said. His phone chimed, and he looked at the screen.

"Maggie, do you follow *SydyBlog*?" he asked.

I remembered Maggie meeting that girl, Sydney when Maggie showed me around the village. I meant to check out that blog but forgot about it.

"No. I haven't read anything on the blog in a long time," Maggie said. "But I know you follow it. Why? What's she writing about now?"

"I got a notification. She just posted something. She's asking people for information about a missing cross."

"What missing cross?" Maggie asked.

Angus passed his phone to Maggie. "Here, it sounds sort of cool. Read it."

I moved my chair closer to Maggie so I could read the post too.

A Black Creek Mystery!

by Sydney Raymond

Help my uncle, Father Joe, make the Church Anniversary Celebration be an even bigger success. If you have any information on the missing Gilded Cross, message me right away!
For the last 40 years, the whereabouts of the church's most valuable possession has been a mystery.
Someone tried to steal the cross from the church back then but failed.

To protect it, the church caretaker hid the cross in an undisclosed location. But the caretaker, the only person who knew of the cross' location, died suddenly. Stay tuned for more to come as I continue to investigate.

"I assumed Sydney was interested in the Church Anniversary Celebration just to help her uncle spread the word," Maggie said. "I should have known there'd be some story or mystery behind it."

"Do you guys know anything about this missing Gilded Cross?" I asked. It seemed like a cool story.

"I've heard about it." Angus said. "My mom's talked about it a few times. Other than that, only what Sydney posted. The Gilded Cross disappeared way before we were born. My mom said something about people breaking into the church back then and trying to steal it. And that nobody could figure out what ended up happening to it."

"Maybe Sydney will figure it out," I said.

"Maybe," Angus said. "I'll keep following her blogs about it for sure."

Soon after, we finished our lattes and headed back to Angus' house. We figured the coast would be clear of Rodney and his gang by then.

Chapter Thirteen

I picked up my pace on my way home that evening. It was getting dark, and Mom was expecting me any minute.

Maggie, Angus, and I swam in Angus's pool all afternoon until it rained. Then Angus and I played video games and had dinner after Maggie left for her guitar practice. As usual, Angus' house was so much fun that I lost track of time and I stayed longer than I was supposed to.

I could have taken the longer route home through the park, but the grass was wet, and I didn't want to walk through the park alone. The other option was to take the main street and walk by the creepy church. I tried my luck with the church.

"Maybe nothing will happen this time," I thought.

I crossed to the opposite side of the road from the church, pulling my hoodie up over my head. I kept my eyes on the sidewalk and everything was fine until a reflection of light in a puddle caught my attention. I couldn't help myself and looked up to see where it was coming from.

It was the church tower window again. The brightness cut through the darkening sky like a tractor beam pulling me in. I couldn't help but answer its call and turned to face the source.

I didn't have a choice, or at least it felt that way.

But why? What was the big deal about a light in a window? I just had to look away from the window and keep walking.

Suddenly a face appeared through the glass, a man, looking right down at me! Then I recognized him. It was the same old man who had looked in my bedroom window. He had that same intense stare. His thin lips were moving, but no sound was coming out, and this time, he was coming for me!

He floated out of the window like a cloud of smoke.

Startled, I stepped back and stumbled but regained my balance. This couldn't be happening! Could it? I looked around. Was anyone else seeing this? A couple walked by me, chatting. They didn't seem to notice a thing.

The billowy figure was coming closer and closer.

I ran as fast as I could, my heart pounding. I didn't know if it was possible to outrun a ghost, but I was sure going to try.

I felt the old man behind me, chasing me, so I ran even faster, those intense eyes fixed on my every step.

I crossed Black Creek Road without checking for traffic and a car horn blared at me. I didn't care. That stare, those eyes, they crawled up my spine like spiders.

I passed the beauty salon and the General Store. Still running, I dared to look back.

I couldn't see the ghost but I wasn't getting off that easy.

"Hheeelllppp! Hheeeeellllppp!" a voice called.

He was still after me and I could hear him.

A group of villagers on the Daily Ground patio were enjoying the cool evening as I whizzed by, knocking over an empty café chair.

A man shouted, "Hey! Slow down, kid!"

I ignored him. I still couldn't see the old man, but I kept running, making a left turn onto a path that connected to my street.

"Hheeelllppp! Hheeeeellllppp!" The voice repeated over and over and over.

I kept running. A dog barked in a neighbor's yard.

I can make it, I told myself, but I was almost out of breath. My body wanted me to stop, but sheer willpower kept me moving.

I made another left turn onto my street. I rounded the corner and my house appeared in the distance. A final surge of energy propelled me forward up the porch steps. I burst through the door, ran up the stairs to my room, jumped into bed, and pulled the blankets over my head.

"Jamie!" Mom called from downstairs. "You're home?"

"Yes, Mom!"

I peeked out from under the bedclothes, expecting the old man to be hovering over me or standing beside my bed. There was nothing there except for the happy faces on my wallpaper, smiling at me. For once, I was just as happy to see them.

CHAPTER FOURTEEN

I rubbed the sleep from my eyes as sunshine poured in through my window the next morning. The old man's face had haunted my dreams. I shivered remembering him flying out of the window at me and chasing me home.

I made my way downstairs, still in my pajamas. Janine was sitting at the kitchen island texting.

"Good morning, boil butt." She looked up from her phone and grinned before taking a sip of her coffee. Janine always looked like she was on the verge of laughing at me.

I reached into the fridge, grabbed the orange juice, and poured myself a glass, not bothering with a comeback.

"What do you and your little zitty friends have going on today?"

"Why would I tell you?"

I felt like I had the same conversations with her over and over again. Maybe I needed to add déjà vu to the list of bizarre things happening to me.

"Fine. Don't tell me. I'm sure Marian will be very interested to know you wouldn't cooperate," Janine said as she walked out of the room.

I called after her.

"I'm going to Maggie's house, and then we might hang out with Angus and play basketball."

"Fine," Janine said. "By the way, Grandma is coming to visit this weekend. She called while you were out last night."

I nodded.

Maybe I could talk to Grandma about the old man's ghost. He was freaking me out. I couldn't believe that I'd seen him twice in such detail, and I'd heard his voice too. Maybe I was seeing him with the special sight Grandma said could help people, but that seemed crazy! How could I help him? I didn't even know who he was or what he wanted.

I wish I had some other gift or talent. Why couldn't I be good at the violin or something?

It was so confusing. Should I wait and talk to Grandma? Or should I tell Maggie and Angus? Maybe they could help me figure it out.

PING! A text.

Maggie
Want to come over?

Perfect timing. Maybe it was a sign.

Me
Yup. Just eating. There soon.

Maggie
OK Hurry! I'm watching a zombie movie.

I finished my orange juice and hurried upstairs to change my clothes. I looked in the mirror and grabbed my hair gel to smooth out that stubborn piece of hair on the side of my head. It was refusing to flatten. I leaned into the mirror to add more gel when...

I froze.

My reflection looked different.

My face was changing and became rounder. Deep wrinkles appeared on my forehead and my cheeks. The hair on the top of my head disappeared and the rest of it turned grey. My eyes changed shape.

This was no longer my face looking back at me.

My reflection had morphed into the old man!

His lips moved, and he whispered. "Jaammiiiieeee! Help!"

I jumped, and as fast as the old man had appeared, he was gone.

It was right then that I made up my mind. I was sick of feeling afraid of my visions, of creeps like Ricky and Rodney, even of Janine and her nastiness.

I had to stop being scared and find out what the old man wanted. Maybe if I did that, I'd finally get some peace.

The first thing I had to do was tell Maggie and Angus about all of this. I was ready. It was stupid to go on keeping this to myself.

Chapter Fifteen

Maggie's basement was a great place to watch movies. The room had two tiny windows, each in a top corner of the rear wall. This left the room dark enough for the TV to glow and reflect light off of the walls.

When I arrived, Maggie's eyes were glued to the screen, her hand lost in Marjorie's thick black fur. The sounds of zombies grunting and gurgling filled the room. Marjorie looked up and acknowledged my arrival before placing her head back on Maggie's lap.

"Hey, Jamie. Guess what? The zombies need to eat people to survive. How predictable!" Maggie rolled her eyes and changed the channel.

"Why can't they ever find a cure? So disappointing! We'll have to find something else to watch."

"Hey, Maggie," I said.

I had to fess up while I still had the nerve. "I have something to tell you." I sat down at the end of the couch.

"What's up? Is something wrong?" She turned down the volume on the TV. "You have a serious look on your face."

I let it all out. I told Maggie about how back in Newbury, I had nightmares, heard voices, and saw things no one else was seeing. She was listening intently, taking it all in. Her face gave little away. I couldn't tell if I shocked her, she was interested, or both. But I continued. I explained that I hoped moving to Black Creek would make it stop, but it didn't. I told her about seeing the old man at the church, outside my bedroom window and in my mirror.

I stopped, took a deep breath, and waited for her reaction.

"What's happening to you sounds very scary!"

"I wish it wasn't, but the truth is, it's scary most of the time," I said.

And then, Maggie's face lit up!

"I knew there was something creepy about the church!"

Maggie's look shifted to disappointment. "Why didn't you tell me about all of this before now?"

"I thought you wouldn't believe me. So, you do?"

"Of course, I believe you! It sounds like you have a super-power, like you're a psychic or something! Maybe you're a real life medium like that famous blonde lady only without the big hair and long nails!"

I laughed and felt myself relax. It made me wonder if I should have tried harder with my Newbury friends. Maybe I was too quick to decide they wouldn't believe me.

"I wouldn't go that far. All I know is that it didn't stop when we moved here, and it's actually gotten worse. And now, I'm scared but, I'm tired of being afraid."

Maggie turned off the TV.

“I get it. It’s fun to talk about strange visions and creepy nightmares when it’s a TV show or a movie. I can’t imagine it happening in actual life!”

“My Grandma calls it a special sight,” I said. “In fact, maybe you have it too. Whenever you walk by the church, you feel something weird, like I do. You could be sensing something.”

It would be great if I wasn’t alone in this. Maggie and I could be a team!

Maggie’s eyes widened.

“But how could this man you’re seeing be connected to the church? Why do you think you keep seeing him?”

“Beats me. That’s what I want to find out. He calls my name and yells for help, and I hide or run. Maybe it’s time I listened.”

“I agree. And I need to find out if I have this special sight.”

BAH! BAH! BAH!

It was the alarm on my phone again!

Chapter Sixteen

"It's doing it again!" I said, holding up my phone. "It can't be a coincidence that it went off right when we were talking about the ghost."

"That's weird," Maggie said, standing up. Marjorie meowed in protest at being disturbed and jumped off the couch.

"Come on! Let's talk to Angus. We'll figure out what to do together. This is exciting! A Black Creek paranormal mystery to solve."

I didn't waste any time when we got to Angus's house. Maggie and I stood in his room while he sat at his desk and listened. I revealed my whole story, including seeing the ghost of the old man at the church. This time, I felt more comfortable telling it.

A smile appeared on Angus's face.

"This is so cool!" he exclaimed.

Maggie and Angus both believed me! Maybe their interest in the paranormal made it easier for them. Whatever the reason, I wasn't alone anymore.

"What does the old man want help with? And why was he in the tower? There's nothing up there. The church office is in the basement."

Maggie held her hands up in frustration. "Jamie doesn't know that, Angus!"

"How am I supposed to know?" Angus protested. "Wouldn't it be awesome if Maggie and I could see or hear the old man too? Can we check out the church? Not that I don't believe you. I just think it would be fun!"

"That would be cool but are you sure you want to see what I see? And besides, how would we even do that?"

"We can use my App, of course! And we can set up an infrared camera and one of those audio recorders that detects noises and voices made by ghosts. I see it on TV all the time."

"Where are we going to get that stuff?" Maggie asked. "Unless we can figure out a way to borrow some equipment from a group of ghost hunters, I think we're stuck with using your App and whatever other low-tech stuff we can find, like the cameras on our phones."

"That might work," Angus said.

"We can at least try," I said. "Even if we don't have the equipment to record anything, at least the two of you might see or hear something, and I'll know that it's not just me!"

Maybe I could finally get answers. Thanks to Maggie and Angus, my fear was turning into an adventure!

"Let's do it tonight," Angus said.

"Works for me," Maggie said. "As long as it's after my soccer practice."

“Works for me too,” I said.

“In the meantime, Angus, can you look at my phone?” I asked, pulling it out of my back pocket. “The alarm went off again for no reason.”

“Sure. Leave it with me. I’ll check it out,” he said, taking my phone. “But first, let’s go to the General Store. I need to get a new charger. I want to make sure my phone is ready for tonight.”

Maggie, Angus, and I headed off. We cut through the park, talking about our plans for the evening.

“Let’s meet at my house at 8:30 tonight,” I said. “We’ll go to the church from there.”

Angus and Maggie agreed.

As we passed through the picnic area, I saw Angus’ brother, Donny, holding a basketball and sitting on a picnic table with Rodney and Ricky. Janine was there too. She had met a bunch of girls who seemed to be as mean as her, and the gang of them were hanging out with the three boys. Janine was giggling and tossing her blond hair around at Rodney.

My face flushed with embarrassment and I groaned. “Oh, ick!”

How could my sister like a guy like Rodney? He was such a jerk!

“Since when does your sister hang out with my brother and his nasty friends?”

“Who knows?” I asked.

Janine’s girlfriends would come and go from our house, giggling and doing boring things like reading fashion magazines and making fun of the models and actresses.

"How can she wear something like that?" Brittany would ask.

"I know! She looks so fat in those pants," Janine would snicker.

"And that is the worst fake tan, like ever!" Kendra would say.

The girls almost never said hi to me. I didn't care if they spoke to me or not, because if they did, they'd just be nasty anyway.

So, I didn't pay much attention to Janine and her friends. But I was pretty sure this was the first time I'd seen them hanging out with Donny and his gang.

"It looks like she has a thing for Rodney Bucci," Angus said.

"Ew!" Maggie said, turning up her nose. "That is so gross."

"I don't feel like getting picked on. Can we walk around them?" I asked.

"We'd have to turn around and it would too obvious. Besides, we're almost there. Let's just look busy," Angus said. He glanced at his phone, and Maggie and I pretended to be having a serious conversation.

We walked past the group, looking preoccupied and hoping to make it to the opposite end of the park without a confrontation.

But no such luck.

"Well, well, well," Rodney Bucci sneered. "The nerd patrol is back!"

I hoped his comment would be the end of it, but then the other kids laughed at us, including Donny and Janine.

I shot Janine an angry look, and Angus did the same to Donny.

Janine caught my eye and mouthed, "What?" She and Donny exchanged looks and then looked away. Clearly neither of them were planning to speak up and defend us.

Rodney walked over to Angus and looked down at Angus' phone. "Hey, what have you got there? Let me see that!"

"No," Angus declared. "It's mine."

Rodney mocked Angus and sneered. "It's mmiiiinnne"

"Hand it over, loser!" Rodney grabbed the phone out of Angus's hands before Angus could put it in his pocket. Rodney pulled the antenna out of the phone. "What little nerdy thing is stuck in here?"

"We'd explain to you, but there are too many big boy words for you to understand," Maggie said.

My eyes widened and I looked over at Maggie. She was glaring at Rodney, fists clenched. Wow! She's brave!

Rodney scowled back at Maggie and turned to Angus. "This is a crappy old version of this phone. It's garbage."

He was about to throw it into the bushes when Donny interrupted.

"Rodney, leave them alone. We need to finish our basketball game."

Rodney laughed. "Fine." He carelessly handed the phone back to Angus.

"Get out of here, nerds. Don't forget that I'm watching you!"

Rodney then purposely tossed the antenna over Angus' head and it landed on the ground behind him. Angus turned around, crouched down, and felt the surrounding grass while Rodney and his friends laughed. Angus found the antenna and stood up.

Donny looked at Angus and mouthed, “Just go home.”

My face reddened with anger. At least Donny said something to help his brother. Janine had just stood there!

“Those creeps make me so mad!” Maggie said.

“Let’s just forget them and get to the store,” I said. “We have work to do.”

Chapter Seventeen

Angus pedaled up my driveway that evening. He joined Maggie and I on my front porch, huffing.

"I rode here as fast as I could. I'm dying to use my App!"

"This is super exciting!" Maggie said.

"Wait," I said. "Angus, do you have my phone?"

"Yep. I looked up the problem, and it's a bug." Angus unzipped the front pocket of his backpack. "I downloaded an update. It should be fine now."

He handed me my phone.

"Thanks, Angus."

I was almost disappointed that my phone wasn't possessed. I didn't think the explanation could be that simple, but I put it out of my mind, eager to get to the church.

I grabbed my bike and climbed on. "We should get going."

A short time later, we stopped and parked our bikes in the bike rack in the vacant lot across the street from the church.

Maggie pointed at a row of green bushes with tiny white

flowers that grew between the sidewalk and the road.

"This is perfect! Those bushes are tall and thick enough to hide in. If something happens in the church tower, we won't miss it."

"I brought snacks," Angus said. He opened his bulging backpack to reveal potato chips, granola bars, two boxes of crackers, bananas, apples, and about six juice boxes. "Help yourselves!"

"Thanks Angus, but how hungry do you think we're going to get?" I asked. "Dinner wasn't that long ago."

"We need to eat." Angus zipped his backpack shut. "This is a stakeout like in the movies where the cops sit in their cars, eat donuts, and wait for the bad guys to do something wrong!"

"You watch too much TV!" Maggie said.

"The sun is going down," I said. "Let's get into position."

We got down on our hand and knees and crawled into the bushes on our elbows, pushing branches aside and positioning ourselves shoulder to shoulder on our stomachs to get the best view of the tower. Maggie was sandwiched between Angus and I. She held up her phone and pointed it directly at the tower window, ready to record any sounds or activity. Angus inserted the antenna into his phone and opened his new app.

Minutes passed like hours. Darkness started to fall while we watched with quiet anticipation.

"This is taking forever!" Angus complained. He unzipped his backpack and pulled out a bag of potato chips. "I could play a game or something to pass the time. I just downloaded a new one this morning."

"Ssshhhh!" I said. "Keep watching!"

Angus crunched on his potato chips. "Hey, did I tell you I asked my mom about the church robbery after we read Sydney's blog post? She said the kids who tried to break in went to her high school."

"Shush, Angus!" Maggie said. "Tell us later! We don't have time for one of your stories right now. Keep watching!"

Angus put his chips away with a frown.

A light went on the tower. It flickered and then it vanished.

"Did you guys see that?" Maggie whispered.

"Yes!" I said, my eyes riveted on the light in the window. "The light has the same eerie glow as the other night when I saw the old man in the tower!"

"What? What? I didn't see a light," Angus said. "And my App isn't picking up anything! Maybe it's out of range."

"SSSSHHHHHHH!" Maggie and I hissed in unison.

"Did either of you see anyone go into the church while we've been here?" I asked.

PING! PING!

Maggie's phone chimed, and so did mine.

It was a group text from Angus:

Angus
No, and there's no back door.

"Angus, why are you texting? We're right here beside you," Maggie asked, annoyed.

"You guys said I was being too loud!"

Maggie ignored him.

"There's only a front door and a side door. The church was dark when we got here."

My pulse quickened as we continued watching the tower. My shoulders were hurting from propping myself up on my elbows but I stayed put, fixated on the window.

Minutes passed. The light flickered again and then stayed on.

"There! Does anyone see that?" I asked.

"Yes, I see it!" Maggie said, holding her phone higher, still filming.

"I see it too!" Angus said. "But maybe it's just an electrical problem in the room or something. I have a lamp at home that once turned on all by itself."

Maggie chuckled, eyes still riveted on her screen. "Maybe there's a ghost in your house. Ask it to haunt Donny and his jerky friends!"

"I hope so! I'd record it and start an online video channel."

"That would be so funny! Donny and his friends would be scared for once," I said.

It was so great having Maggie and Angus to help me. I felt like a normal kid for the first time in a long time.

There was a flash of movement in the window and then a man appeared and sat down, possibly at a table or desk. He was facing us but looking down.

"Do you guys see that man?" I asked. Was this the moment when someone would finally see what I saw?

"Yes, and I can see right through him! I think that's a ghost," Maggie said.

"I don't see anyone. No fair!" Angus protested. "All I see is that creepy light, and my App still isn't picking up on anything."

"Ssssshhhhhhhh!" Maggie and I hissed, eyes glued to the tower.

We watched and watched, waiting for the man to do something, afraid to blink or even to breathe.

Then he moved. He held up a piece of paper and seemed to inspect it.

"What's he doing?" I asked. "Is he reading?"

"Maybe he's trying to find something," Maggie said.

"I think that's the old man I've been seeing. I'm not positive, though. He needs to look up."

As if on cue, the man lifted his head and then glanced back down at the papers.

"That's him! That's the old man. Are you getting this on your phone, Maggie?" I asked, not daring to tear my eyes away from the window.

"Yes, I am."

"I wonder what he's looking for?" I asked. I pushed a branch away and shifted forward to see if I could get a better view.

"How come I can't see anything?" Angus whined.

The old man looked up again. He gazed out the window and stared right at us with those black eyes and that intense stare.

"I'm getting out of here!" Maggie cried.

Chapter Eighteen

Maggie crawled out of the bushes with Angus and I close behind.

"Angus, your house is closest. Let's go there!" I said.

Angus nodded, and we hopped on our bikes and raced to his house.

"I've never been so happy to see your gross room and dirty socks, Angus!" Maggie said. Roofus barked as he followed us into the bedroom. "I can't believe what I just saw! I don't think I want this special sight of yours, Jamie. Do you see stuff like that all the time?"

"Not exactly stuff like that. These visions I've had of the old man are more intense than anything I've seen before. But yeah, I've had scary visions lots of times. It started last year."

"I wish I could have seen what you guys saw, even if it was scary," Angus said. "I only saw that light, which was pretty spooky, but it could have been anything. My App didn't detect any electro-magnetic energy." He said and plopped down onto his desk chair, looking defeated.

"You believe we saw a ghost though, don't you?" Maggie asked.

"I guess so," Angus said. "I think we were too far away for my antenna to work, anyway."

"Why don't we look at the video you took, Maggie?" I asked. "Maybe it recorded what we saw, and then Angus can see it too."

Maggie handed Angus her phone. He plugged it into his computer and opened the video. We watched as the church tower appeared on screen. The distinct sound of crunching potato chips blasted through the speakers. Maggie and I glared at Angus.

"What? Sorry! I was hungry," Angus said. "I put them away, remember?"

Maggie sighed, and we directed our attention back to the computer screen. The light flickered and came on in the tower window, just like we'd witnessed.

"I saw that," Angus said.

The video continued to show the tower window, but the light didn't seem so eerie on the screen. Not only that, but the old man never appeared.

"Are you guys sure you saw something else?" Angus asked.

"I don't get it," I said, confused. "Maggie and I both saw him!"

"It's so weird!" Maggie said. "There was definitely something spooky going on in that tower room. I've seen ghosts show up in online videos and on TV shows, so why wouldn't it show up on this video?"

We went through the video again and again in case we'd missed something, but it was the same each time. A light came on in the window and that was it. No ghost.

Realizing how late it was, Maggie and I left and rode our bikes home in silence, stopping at the end of my driveway.

"I'm sorry I didn't record the ghost, but that was the most fun I've had all summer! Seeing the ghost was really scary. But trying to solve the mystery is fun!"

"Yeah," I said, "It's fun with you and Angus helping. It's not as scary as it is when I'm alone."

"That's good," Maggie said with a smile.

She paused. "This is all new for me, and for Angus, but I wonder why you and I could see the ghost, but Angus couldn't."

"I wish I knew," I said.

"Oh, well! At least we're doing something to solve this." Maggie said. "Gotta go. Good night."

"Good night, Maggie." I went inside and directly to my room.

Things had changed for me so much since the beginning of August. After months of feeling afraid, I was finally figuring out what was happening to me but I was still confused. Why would the ghost appear to Maggie and I and then when we looked at the video it was like it never happened?

I sat down on my bed and looked at my Dad's photo on my bedside table. Dad's words were now making sense to me.

"Sometimes, you find solutions to your problems through hard work and determination," he'd often say to me when I had problems at school. But I didn't listen back then.

He'd also say, "check, check, and triple check your answers," when he was helping me with my homework. It was annoying when I just wanted to get my homework done fast.

However, I was going to take Dad's advice this time and grabbed my phone from my bedside table. Maggie sent the video of the tower to Angus and I before we left Angus's house. I opened the video file and pressed play. The familiar image of the church tower appeared. I advanced the video to the spot just before the light in the tower window came on. Maybe we'd missed something.

I studied the each frame as the window lit up, giving off that familiar eerie glow. I kept watching, hoping for some clue about the ghost.

The light got stronger and stronger, causing me to squint. It flickered twice, just like it had when we were there.

I brought the phone closer to my face and—

BAH! BAH! BAH! BAH!

I jumped at the sound, dropping my phone onto the floor. Angus hadn't fixed it after all! I knew it wasn't just a bug.

But when I grabbed the phone and looked at the screen again, I saw the old man.

I knew he'd been there! On the video, he sat down at the desk and looked at papers, just like Maggie and I had witnessed.

I enlarged the image to look at his face. I kept watching intently.

He took one of the papers, stood up and looked straight at me. My heart pounded. That hadn't happened earlier!

The ghost slapped the paper against the windowpane. On it was a message written in capital letters:

FIND THE MAP.

Chapter Nineteen

"What did you see again?" Angus asked, digging his spoon into his cereal bowl. He was eating breakfast at his kitchen table when Maggie and I rushed over to his house. It was late when I texted Maggie and Angus the night before about my alarm and what I'd seen in the video. The biggest surprise for them was the message about the map. Maggie and I talked about it that morning and then quickly rode our bikes over to Angus' house to regroup and plan.

"It was a message," I repeated. "It said, Find the Map."

"A map! Now it's getting interesting!" Angus said.

"Because it wasn't interesting before, Angus?" Maggie asked, sarcastically.

"Can we search online to see what comes up?" I asked. "Maybe there's a story somewhere about this old man and the church."

"Good idea," Angus said. He got up from the table, leaving his cereal bowl behind. Maggie and I followed him to his room.

Angus grabbed his laptop from his desk, sat down on his bed and opened his browser.

"By the way, I swear I thought I fixed your phone," he said.

Maggie and I took a seat on either side of him and looked over his shoulders as he typed 'Old man and Black Creek' into the search engine. Pages and pages of search results appeared.

"You didn't put the word 'church' in there. Be more specific!" Maggie said in a huff. 'Try 'Black Creek church' and add 'mystery'."

Angus made the changes. The first few results weren't helpful. He scrolled down the page. About halfway down the first page was a hit entitled "Local Church Volunteer Passes Away."

"Oh, that's the article that Sydney posted on her blog early this morning. I haven't read it yet. It could be something useful for us," Angus pointed out.

He clicked on the link and opened *SydyBlog*.

"First, there's a comment from Sydney." He read it aloud:

> I promised there was more to come on the investigation into the missing Gilded Cross. I found this article, which is a new piece of the puzzle. If you have any information, message me while I continue my quest to find the missing cross! It would be great if we found it for the Church Anniversary Celebration Labor Day weekend.

"And then," Angus went on, "the article is from the Black Creek Sun from almost 30 years ago. It's dated March 8,

1994. He read aloud again:

LOCAL CHURCH VOLUNTEER PASSES AWAY

'A local Black Creek man was found unconscious in the church office at St. Bartholomew Anglican Church yesterday. Randall McPhee, 63, was a frequent volunteer at the Black Creek church and a local farmer. He was rushed to the hospital but was pronounced dead on arrival.

Randall McPhee is known around town for scaring away two burglars that he caught in the church during a robbery attempt last month. The robbers were about to steal the church's cherished Gilded Cross. McPhee called the police and the burglars were later arrested. 'The Gilded Cross is a large Spanish-style solid gold cross with diamonds, rubies, and emeralds. It was a gift from the local bishop when the church opened in 1853. After the robbery attempt, McPhee was tasked with protecting the Gilded Cross, the church's most valuable and cherished holy item. McPhee lived alone and, apparently in order to protect the cross, it seems he may not have revealed its hiding place to anyone. With McPhee's passing, the search has begun for the Gilded Cross.

"And that's the end," Angus said.

"Why didn't you say anything about this before, Angus?" Maggie asked. "This might be important. Now we know the name of the caretaker, Randall McPhee, and that he was a volunteer who died in the church."

"Hey, I hadn't read Sydney's blog, yet. I was eating breakfast!"

"Fine," Maggie said. "At least we know about it now."

I was too excited to care about Maggie and Angus' arguing. I looked over Angus' shoulder. "Maybe the ghost in the tower is Randall McPhee! Maybe he's trying to tell us where the Gilded Cross is!"

"Is there a photo of Randall McPhee anywhere?" Maggie asked.

"No photo," Angus said.

"Is there a section we're missing, Angus? I asked "Is there anything about why he was in the church tower room in the first place? The article says that he was found in the church office. I thought you told me the church office is in the basement."

"It is now. Maybe the office was in the tower back then," Angus speculated.

"We need to find out more. Let's search his name," I suggested.

Angus typed in the name 'Randall McPhee' and started a new search. The *SydyBlog* article we had just read came up on the first page, but there was nothing else. Angus clicked on page two and found nothing.

"Let's try searching *SydyBlog* directly," Maggie said.

Angus immediately found another scanned article that Sydney had posted. It was also from the Black Creek Sun but dated April 16th, 1994, a month after the first article.

"Looks like Sydney's on the case!" he said.

Maggie and I read the article, still peering over Angus' shoulders. The beginning paragraphs repeated information we already knew, but then added a few extra details.

"Father Joe asked McPhee to hide the Gilded Cross until the church could raise enough money for security to protect it. As part of his duties, McPhee would bring the cross to each mass. He would return it to safekeeping afterwards.

Now, the cross is nowhere to be found. It appears Randall McPhee took the secret of its hiding-place to his grave. McPhee passed away with no sign of where the cross could be. Father Joe, thinking the hiding place was only temporary, never asked McPhee where the cross was hidden. Father Joe stated, “It was better I didn’t know for security reasons. The police searched the McPhee farm and found nothing.”

It finished with a request for anyone with any information on the location of the cross to contact the Black Creek police.

“Randall McPhee must be the ghost, the old man!” I said. “Who else could it be?”

“How can we be sure it’s him?” Angus asked.

Suddenly, the floor just outside the room creaked. Angus’ bedroom door was open a crack.

Someone was in the hallway listening.

CHAPTER TWENTY

I nudged Angus, and then Maggie, and pointed at the door.

"Donny, is that you?" Angus asked.

"Uh, no, it's Ricky."

Ricky pushed the door open and looked in.

"Donny and I were just looking for your basketball."

"It's in the garage where it always is!" Angus snapped.

"It's not in the garage. We already looked there."

I spotted the basketball under a pile of dirty clothes and picked it up.

"He's right, Angus. It's here. You couldn't see it underneath this pile. Gross!"

Angus grabbed the basketball from me and handed it to Ricky. He closed the door and sat down, returning to his computer screen.

"Maybe Sydney knows more than she's blogging about," I said, getting back to the task at hand.

“Can we ask Sydney what else she knows?” Maggie asked.

“We can ask her in the comments section of her blog,” Angus said. “She said she wants people to message her if they know anything.”

“But we don’t know anything, Angus,” Maggie pointed out. “Are you going to tell her about the ghost?”

“No, I’m just going to ask her a question.” He started typing a message as Maggie and I looked on.

"Hey Sydney - Angus Fisher here. What else do you know about Randall McPhee? Do you have a photo of him?"

“Maybe we can find out more on our own in the meantime,” I said. “Could we check out that tower room and look around? There could be more clues in there.”

“I doubt we’re allowed up there,” Maggie said. “And even if we were, what reason would we give for snooping around?”

“We’ll have to sneak in,” Angus concluded. He stood up from his desk chair. It was getting stuffy in his room, so he opened his window.

“But what if we get caught or, worse, run into that old man’s ghost?” Maggie asked. “I’m not sure what I’ll do if I see that again! Scream probably! Besides, how can we get up there? They lock the church when it’s not being used.”

“I have a Youth Group meeting there tomorrow night at seven,” Angus said. “We talk about church stuff and we sing a lot, but maybe I can find something out.”

“Can Maggie and I come?” I asked. “Not to the meeting, though. Maybe one of us could sneak up into the tower when no one is looking.”

"Um, I guess so," Angus said. He thought for a minute. "I know! Maggie, you have soccer practice on my youth group nights, but it's at 5.30, right? I think you finish up before my group starts. So, what if you both meet me at the church at seven o'clock? Jamie, we won't let anyone see you, but I'll tell Mrs. Pruit, the leader of our group, that Maggie wants to join. While she's being introduced and no one is looking, Jamie can try to sneak into the tower room."

"So, I guess I'll be the one who might see the ghost. Thanks a lot!" I was kidding, but only sort of. "Maybe if we know for sure who the ghost is, it'll make it less scary."

"Okay, I'll ask my Dad to drop me off at the church tomorrow night. Jamie, you can meet us there," Maggie said. "Just don't expect me to become a permanent member of your Youth Group, Angus!"

"It's a deal!" Angus said.

Maggie, Angus, and I had gone for a swim at Angus's and hung out at the park for the rest of the afternoon. I got home just in time for dinner and took my seat at the table. Janine and Mom had filled their plates with steak and salad.

"It's about time you got here, pus face!" Janine said.

Mom gave her a look of warning.

I ignored Janine and cut through my steak.

"I did text you, Jamie," Mom said. "You're late a lot these days!"

"I know! I'm sorry! I was having fun with my friends."

"The nerd patrol kept you busy?" Janine asked.

"Janine!" Mom said.

I looked at Janine. "Why are you hanging out with those losers at the park, anyway?" I asked.

"They're not losers. You and your little baby friends are the losers," she pushed her salad around on her plate with her fork. "You can't blame people for noticing, by the way. They have eyes! You should thank us for letting you know so you can do something about it."

"Janine! Stop that kind of talk this instant!" Mom ordered.

"Fine, Marian." Janine rolled her eyes.

I wasn't ready to let the conversation end just yet. "You're twisted, Janine. That Rodney Bucci dude is a total jerk!"

Janine's face flushed a bright pink. "You don't know him like I do."

"I'm sure he has a sensitive side that nobody else sees," I chided. "You've known him for all of five minutes!"

Janine kept defending Rodney. "He was just messing with you guys yesterday."

I realized that like most conversations with Janine, this one was also pointless.

"Whatever! It's your life," I said, shoveling a forkful of food into my mouth.

"Get used to it," Janine said. "Rodney Bucci will be coming around here more often. We're going out this week.

I stuck my finger in my mouth, pretending to gag.

"I'll try not to barf."

"Can't you two just be nice to one another?" Mom pleaded.

"I'm going upstairs to plan my outfit for my big date," Janine said, avoiding the question.

"Please stop talking about that!" I said. "I'm losing my appetite."

Janine took her barely touched plate of food into the kitchen, and I stayed to finish my dinner.

After helping Mom clean up, I went up to my room, sat down at my desk, and opened my laptop. I decided I'd do some of my own investigating. I opened the *SydyBlog* to look for anything else about the Gilded Cross and Randall McPhee. No results.

Then I scrolled through the blog posts, just scanning them. It was something I'd been wanting to do since that first day in Black Creek when I met Sydney. Several of Sydney's posts about UFO abductions and faked interviews from space caught my eye.

"You can see the cable holding him up while the astronaut is supposed to be floating across the back of the space station," she wrote.

Sydney also posted articles about unsolved crimes and local hauntings, but nothing else about the cross. Well, at least we hadn't missed anything.

I was curious to learn more about Sydney herself. Other than what Maggie had told me, I knew little about her. I rarely ever saw her around the village. I clicked on a tab that said "About Me," in the upper right-hand corner of her website. She described herself as "a truth-seeking investigative blogger." She went on: "If there's a cover-up, mystery, or unsolved crime, I will ask the right questions. But I don't just ask them, I investigate and dig deep to find the answers. When I get those answers, I share them with the world even if the world isn't ready to hear them."

Sydney was even cooler than I thought! We should try to hang out with her.

I went back to scouring for more clues. What could I search next? I had an idea! Maybe there was something in those articles about a ghost in the church tower. I clicked on the Hauntings tab and found a recent post, speculating that the abandoned toy factory in the village was haunted. Underneath, a woman with the account name "Clean4U" had written a comment. She said she knew nothing about the factory, but five years ago, she was in the church one night, cleaning the bathrooms. A door slammed at the back of the church and she heard someone going up and down the stairs. She wrote:

> *"The old office in the tower room isn't used so there's no reason for anyone to be up there. When I came out to check what was causing the noise, there was nobody there."*

I knew we couldn't be the only ones who had contact with the ghost in the tower! And the church office was originally in the Tower, like Angus had guessed.

I couldn't wait to tell my Maggie and Angus.

"A new clue!"

CHAPTER TWENTY-ONE

The Youth Group met every Thursday evening. Mrs. Pruit, a local woman who, according to Angus, knew everything about everyone in Black Creek, hosted it. She worked at the library and ran several church and volunteer groups in the village. If someone moved into town, she knew who they were, where they came from, and practically what their blood type was! Angus said she made sure she volunteered everywhere so that she never missed a second of potential gossip.

As arranged, Maggie, Angus and I met outside the church right before the Youth Group meeting. Maggie was still in her soccer uniform.

I had texted Maggie and Angus first thing that morning about the comment I had found posted by the cleaning lady on the *SydyBlog*.

Maggie replied right away.

Maggie
At least we know it isn't just us that thinks something paranormal is happening at the church.

I was glad Maggie shared my relief about that.

Me
And now we know for sure that the church office used to be in the tower

Even though Maggie and I were coming to the same conclusions, Angus seemed to have doubts.

Angus
I guess. But it could have been anything making that noise. Maybe the lady was hearing the priest or something. We still need to search the room in the tower to see if there are any clues in there.

I figured that it would be better to continue our conversation in person later that morning.

Me
Okay. See you later.

We huddled off to one side to go over our plan. Angus took the lead and whispered, "Our group meets in the church's nave. That's where the altar is and the pews. Jamie, remember you're going to sneak in and wait at the very back of the nave. When I introduce Maggie, follow along the back wall. Keep to your left until you get to the opening at the back corner. That's where the bathrooms are and the staircase that leads to the tower room. I know every inch of the church! I take as many bathroom breaks as I can during these boring meetings."

"How do you know the stairs lead to the tower room?" I asked.

"Because I snuck up there once a few years ago during one of those breaks. I remember seeing a door at the top of the stairs. That's as far as I got though. I was afraid of getting caught. There's nothing else up there so that has to be the room."

"Okay. I'll try to get up there and check it out," I said.

"Don't forget, Maggie. If Mrs. Pruit doesn't introduce you to the others, I will."

"Got it, Angus. Jamie, what if you get caught walking around up there?"

I hadn't thought about what I would say. Then it came to me. "I'll just say I'm looking for the priest's office, and that someone told me it was up there. It was the old office, remember?"

"Good idea!" Angus said. "But be careful. Get your story straight. If you get caught and Mrs. Pruit doesn't believe you, she'll tell your mom and you'll end up having to go to the Youth Group meetings every week. Mrs. Pruit will make sure of that!"

"I hope that's the worst thing that happens!" I said.

"Are you ready, Jamie?" Maggie asked.

"Yep!" But was I? My pulse quickened at the thought of seeing that old man from my nightmares again. I knew I had to face my fears if I wanted to find any answers that might be hiding in the church tower room.

The kids in the Youth Group began arriving and heading inside. I stayed out of sight at the side of the church while Maggie and Angus walked up the stone steps to the front door. They wanted to be the last ones in so I could slip into the foyer behind them without being noticed. Maggie and Angus waited at the door until everyone else had gone inside to take their seats. When they walked into the foyer, that was my cue, and I ducked inside behind them. And when they moved from the foyer into the main part of the church, what Angus called the nave, I stayed in the back in the shadows, out of sight, waiting until the coast was clear.

This was the first time I had been inside of the church. It looked old, with sections of wooden pews in rows, all facing an impressive altar. Dark mahogany walls enclosed the altar. Multi-colored beams of sunlight streamed in through tall rectangular stained-glass windows, and a fresco of clouds and chubby blond baby angels covered the ceiling.

I pictured Randall McPhee, along with hundreds, maybe thousands, of other villagers, coming and going, sitting in those pews over the years. I could see why the church wanted to celebrate the anniversary.

I focused my attention on the kids and Mrs. Pruit, waiting for my signal to move across the back of the church. Mrs. Pruit was a tall, overweight woman, younger than Grandma but older than Mom. Her long greying dark hair was tied back loosely in a ponytail. Metal blue-rimmed round glasses sat on the tip of her large nose. She was handing out pamphlets to the kids. They all looked ten years old or older. Some waited quietly, and others were talking amongst themselves. Maggie and Angus joined the group at the front of the church and turned to face Mrs. Pruit.

"Last to arrive again, Angus Fisher!" Mrs. Pruit said.

"Sorry, Mrs. Pruit. I've brought my friend Maggie with me today."

"Hello, Maggie. Zhou, is it? I don't see your family here at church on Sundays."

"We don't go to church very often, Mrs. Pruit."

"Hm. I gathered as much. "Well, you're here now. Everyone, please welcome Maggie to our gathering this evening"

I got ready.

As Angus predicted, all eyes turned to Maggie when Mrs. Pruit introduced her, and as they did, Maggie gave me a quick nod. That was my cue.

"Hi, Maggie," the group said in unison. I snuck out of the shadows of the foyer and tiptoed across the rear of the church, as planned.

"So far, so good," I whispered.

I continued along the back wall to the room with the washrooms and the narrow staircase to the tower room. Angus's directions were perfect.

Grabbing the railing, I took slow, deliberate steps up the three stairs at the base of the staircase, listening for creaks. From the first landing, the staircase veered sharply to the left. I continued my slow climb, leaving footprints behind me in the thick dust. It was obvious nobody went up there often. Maybe Angus was the last person to use these stairs.

I reached a spacious landing at the top of the stairs and was facing a wooden door with a wide frame and a transom above it, just like Grandma had at her house. I had asked her once why she had windows above her doors, and she told me they were an old-fashioned way to circulate air through a house or building.

What if they locked the door? I grabbed the doorknob and— phew! — I could turn it. But when I tried to push it open, the door wouldn't budge. I turned the knob again and pushed on the door with more force. It still didn't move! I tried once again, throwing my weight against it with a thump.

Had anyone heard that? If anyone came to investigate, it would ruin our entire plan.

I listened, certain that someone would check out the noise.

Nobody came. I sighed with relief and, emboldened, threw my shoulder against the door again. It finally budged. One more try, and the door opened wide.

CHAPTER TWENTY-TWO

I walked into the room, pushed the door closed, and sneezed from the cloud of dust that rose from all the movement. The cloud settled, and I had a clear view of a tiny room with white walls that were yellowing with age. Chunks of missing plaster exposed the wooden slats underneath. Loose wires hung from the ceiling where a light fixture used to be. The room obviously hadn't been used in a very long time—so why did I feel like I'd been there before?

A brown wooden desk and chair sat under the window. Four large cardboard boxes were stacked in the corner beside the desk. I was certain this was the desk where the ghost had sat. I walked over to it and looked out the window which faced the street. The bushes where the three of us had hidden were in clear view. I could see them clearly. That confirmed that it was the spot where Randall McPhee looked out at us!

He had written "FIND THE MAP" on a piece of paper and he'd been holding several other papers, but the desk had nothing on it except for a small brass lamp. It had one drawer that ran along its entire length, with three smaller drawers underneath on the right-hand side. Each drawer had a separate keyhole.

I held my breath, hoping they'd be unlocked, and tried the long drawer first. I lucked out and it opened. Inside, I found a few old church bulletins and faded store receipts from the 1980s. The smaller top drawer easily slid open but was empty. I tried the middle drawer. It was stuck.

I pulled and shook it several times. Locked! I pulled on the bottom drawer. Also locked.

I needed the keys, but, where were they?

A blast of cold air blew up the back of my shirt and there was a sudden shift in the room's energy.

Goosebumps covered my arms like a sheath.

My warm breath looked like small clouds of smoke.

I leaned over the desk and checked the window to see if it was open. It was tightly closed.

Then the hairs on the back of my neck stood up as if detecting a force behind me.

I was being watched. I knew it.

I whipped around.

It was the old man, right there in the tower room!

I could almost see through him, but, just like before, his features were visible. Only this time, I could make out the red plaid shirt, denim overalls, and black rubber boots he was wearing. He didn't move. He stared right at me with those intense eyes.

We were only a few feet from one another, frozen in a silent standoff.

The old man made the first move.

He slowly lifted his arm and pointed at the boxes stacked

in the corner. Then he turned and walked away, right through the wall!

The room immediately warmed up again.

I grabbed the desk chair and sat down heavily on it, emptying my lungs in relief. I knew I might see the ghost, but I was glad it was over.

He pointed at the boxes. The old man was trying to tell me something, but what?

When my heart rate went back to normal, I pushed my fear aside and headed for the boxes. I grabbed the one resting on the top of the stack. I wasn't expecting it to be heavy, and it fell out of my hands, hitting the floor loudly.

Darn!

I tiptoed to the door and put my ear against it, listening for the sound of footsteps on the stairs. Nothing.

I returned to the boxes.

The box I'd dropped had books called Sunday Missals inside. I moved on to the next one, lifting it off the stack. It contained envelopes for church donations and some old church paperwork in file folders. I removed the files and fished through the remaining envelopes and papers scattered around the box. One of the church donation envelopes wouldn't move. I felt around and found it taped to the bottom.

I pulled at the envelope, and it ripped. Five keys strung around a simple silver key ring fell out. Four of the keys looked almost identical, while one was long and tubular with two square rungs at the tip.

I hurried to the desk and inserted one of the lookalike keys into the keyhole of the locked middle drawer. The key fit, but the lock wouldn't budge.

I tried the second key. It also fit, and when I turned it, the lock clicked. I yanked the drawer open. It was empty except for an old seating chart for the church with a list of local church goers. The McPhee name was on the chart, and the Fisher name.

"Angus's family has lived in Black Creek for a long time!" I murmured.

I unlocked the bottom desk drawer with one of the remaining keys. It held only office supplies and pens and pencils.

My heart sank. I thought for sure I'd find something in there. Why would the ghost point me toward the keys unless they were important? Why would someone hide keys to a desk that had nothing in it worth finding?

Then I remembered seeing investigators on internet videos find hidden compartments and false bottoms in safes, in walls, and even in drawers. I felt around the bottom of each of the desk drawers and found a piece of stiff fabric stuck in the back corner of the last one, like a tab. I pulled on it a few times, and the bottom of the drawer began shifting. I pulled harder and the bottom piece slid right out.

The pens, pencils, and other office supplies dropped onto the actual bottom, landing on an unmarked letter-sized brown envelope the false bottom had hidden.

"Oh, wow!" I said aloud.

I opened the envelope. Inside was a single piece of unfolded paper. On it was a hand drawn image of a large piece of property with a house in the center. Judging by the size of the area, it could have been a farm.

Was this the map in the ghost's message?

Just then I heard a click at the door. I quickly closed the

desk drawers, folded the map, and slipped it and the keys into my back pocket. Looking around for somewhere to hide, I crouched behind the stack of boxes.

I waited.

No one came into the room.

After a few more minutes, I tiptoed over to the door and turned the knob. It was locked. I needed a key to unlock the door from the inside. I tried the long tubular key from the keys that I'd found, but it was too big.

I was locked in!

Chapter Twenty-three

I tried the door handle again.

It didn't budge.

"Who's there?" I asked through the door.

"Stop looking into things that are none of your business!" a voice warned from the other side. "Or else!"

That sounded a lot like Ricky, Rodney Bucci's friend. Why would he lock the door on me? Who even knows that I'm in here?

I tried all the keys I had, hoping one of them would move the lock. No luck. I tried not to panic. But I had to get out of that room! What if the ghost came back? Whether I saw the ghost or not, I didn't want to get caught in this room. Maggie and Angus would eventually rescue me, but that could take a while.

I couldn't yell for help without getting into big trouble. I had to escape.

"Think, think, think!" I said aloud, looking around the

room. "I can't go out the window. It's too high up."

I opened the remaining boxes, which were filled with hymn books. No room to hide a key. Then I noticed the open transom. If I can get up there, I might just fit through it.

I grabbed the desk chair, placed it against the door, and carefully stacked two of the heavier boxes on it.

This could end badly, but I had to try. It was my only option.

I climbed up, putting one hand on the door for support, and stood on the top box, struggling to keep my balance. Thankfully, I was high enough to grab the bottom of the transom sill and pull myself up. I pushed it open wider and poked my head through the gap. I peered down at the floor. Whoever had threatened me was gone.

With my weight on my hands, I slid my shoulders through the window, lifted one leg through the opening and let it hang over the other side of the door. I shifted my body around and then maneuvered the other leg through. The front half of my body was inside of the room and my legs were dangling outside of the room. I wiggled my body until most of it was through the transom. I grabbed the frame with both hands and hung from there for a few seconds, catching my breath. I let go and landed on the floor with a thud.

I gave the knob a quick turn while trying to shake the door. It didn't budge. Someone had definitely locked me in!

A few moments later, I was back downstairs, hiding behind the wall and peeking into the church nave. The Youth Group kids were still gathered at the front. A teenage boy was playing the guitar and Mrs. Pruit was singing a hymn. All that music must have masked the noise I was making upstairs.

Maggie glanced over her shoulder and caught my eye.

"I want out of here!" she mouthed.

I tiptoed through the shadows across the back of the nave and ducked out into the foyer. Then I opened the church door and slipped outside into the cool evening air.

CHAPTER TWENTY-FOUR

I sat on the church steps, waiting for Maggie and Angus. My mind raced with everything that had just happened.

Was it Ricky who locked me in? Why did that room in the tower seem so familiar?

Then, I remembered an old dream, the one from my very first night in Black Creek. That was the room! That was the room in that dream. And there had been people banging on the door, yelling at me.

But, hang on. In my dream, I wasn't locked in the room. Those men wanted something from me, and I'd locked them out.

I had so many questions. The closer we got to finding answers about Randall McPhee and the missing Gilded Cross, the more questions I had.

I took the map and keys out of my pocket and studied them, hoping they might reveal more clues. When I eventually looked up, that kid, Ricky, Donny's friend, was standing across the street, staring at me. He pulled out his phone from the pocket of his hoodie and appeared to be texting someone. It was getting dark, but when he saw that I noticed him, I swear he winked at me. He put his phone back in his pocket, grabbed his bike, and rode away.

The church door opened and Maggie and Angus came out with the rest of the Youth Group members filing out behind them. Mrs. Pruit stood in the doorway and peered over the top of her glasses.

"Shall we expect you again next week, Maggie?"

"I'll have to check with my parents, Mrs. Pruit" Maggie said.

"Well, we would love to have you. Angus, make sure that you're on time next week."

"Yes, Mrs. Pruit."

Maggie, Angus, and I started to walk back to Angus's house.

"I hope you found something, Jamie! I don't want to do that again!" Maggie said. "I don't like to sing and I don't know any of the words to gospel music."

Angus chuckled. "I don't feel bad for you, Maggie. My mom makes me go every Thursday and after church on Sundays. But Jamie, what happened? Did you find anything?"

I excitedly described the night's events, seeing the ghost, finding the map, getting locked in possibly by Ricky, and having to climb out through the transom.

Angus frowned. "You saw the ghost again? I still haven't seen it even once."

"Yep! And it was the same old man. He was tall and dressed like a farmer. He pointed at the boxes to tell me to look inside them. That's where I found the keys for the desk."

"That is cool!" Maggie said. "You were so brave!"

I also told them about how Ricky was watching me across the street from the church and texted someone before taking off on his bike.

"And he winked at me, too," I continued. "He was almost as creepy as the ghost."

"Do you think Ricky locked you in?" Maggie asked. "We didn't notice anyone go back there during the meeting."

"It might have been. It sounded like him, but why would he?"

"Did you see anyone else outside?" Angus asked.

"No. Just Ricky."

"It could just be Ricky playing around. Maybe he was out there and saw you through the tower window and then decided to scare you," Maggie said.

"Well, whoever it was gave me a warning." I said. "How would he have locked the door, anyway? He must have had a key."

"He could have just used a screwdriver or something. Those old locks are pretty big," Angus said. "I doubt it takes much to pick it."

"Hey, guys," Maggie interjected. "Remember when Ricky was at Angus's bedroom door? He said he was looking for the basketball. What if he overheard us talking? He could have listened from outside your bedroom window as well. Maybe he figured out we're trying to solve the mystery of the missing Gilded Cross."

"And he could have come into the church and locked me in the room to scare us away while he tries to find the cross for himself?" I said.

"Yeah, I guess that's possible," Angus said.

Maggie was defiant. “Well, if that’s his plan, it won’t work! We have something he doesn’t, a map. Let’s see it, Jamie.”

“Let’s go to my house and look at the map there,” I said. “We don’t want to bump into Ricky or Rodney, or be overheard again.”

“Ok,” Angus said. “But I can’t stay long. It’s getting late.”

When we arrived, we said a quick hello to Mom and went up to my room. I spread the map out on my desk, careful not to tear it. Maggie and Angus stood beside me, examining it.

“Do you think that could be Randall McPhee’s farm?” Maggie asked.

“I have a feeling that it is,” I said. “Everything that’s happened so far has led us to that room in the tower. I couldn’t find anything else in there that seemed important, except for the keys and the map that the ghost wanted me to find.”

“There aren’t any names or addresses on it. I wonder why,” Maggie said.

“Maybe whoever made the map didn’t finish it,” I guessed.

“Well, let’s see if there’s an address for Randall McPhee online. Then we’ll know,” Angus said.

I opened my laptop and did a quick search. A long list of McPhees came up with addresses from all over the place, but nothing for Black Creek. I refined my search and still, nothing.

“Maybe he lived there before people’s addresses were on the internet,” I said.

“So, let’s assume it’s the ghost’s farm, and that the ghost is Randall McPhee. Doesn’t it mean the cross must be hidden there? Otherwise, why hide the map?” Angus asked. “What’s the big deal about a map of a farm unless the cross is hidden there?”

We looked at each another for a moment. Were we getting close to finding the Gilded Cross?

"But wait. The blog posts said that the police looked for the cross," Maggie said. "If that's Randall McPhee's property, wouldn't they have found the cross if it were there?"

"Or maybe when the police searched for it there, it was too well-hidden and they couldn't find it," I said. "One thing we know is that the map was hidden away for a reason, and we should find out why. I wish this map was more help. It shows the farm, but it doesn't exactly show anything else, nothing that looks like a hiding place."

I held the map up against the light of my desk lamp, and ...

"Hey! Look at this," I said. The direct light from the lamp revealed a path of very faded Xs drawn on the map in pencil, which stopped at a spot on the property behind the farmhouse. The final X was twice the size of the others.

"Wow!" Angus said. "Maybe that's it! Maybe that last X is where Randall McPhee hid the cross! Let's go find it!"

"Whoa, wait a minute," I said. "We can't! Don't forget, we don't even have an address. We don't know where the farm is."

"I know! We can go to the library and look up the old Black Creek records. We should be able to find Randall McPhee's address there," Angus said.

"How will we know it's the same property?" Maggie asked. "There's no name on this map."

"We'll know when we get to the farm," Angus said. "We can compare the actual property to what's drawn on the map."

"It's worth a try," Maggie said. "But the library is closed now."

“I have to go home anyway. My mom just sent me a text,” Angus said.

“We’ll go the library tomorrow morning.” I said. “Angus, make sure that your brother and his friends don’t overhear something about this. Let’s keep it between us.”

“My lips are sealed,” he promised.

CHAPTER TWENTY-FIVE

The library opened early on Fridays to host reading programs for little kids. So, the next morning, Maggie and I rode our bikes over and met Angus out front.

"Hey guys," Angus greeted us. "When I got home last night, Donny asked me a lot of questions about what we're up to. And Ricky and Rodney were over and kept giving me funny looks. They may be on to us. I don't think they know much but we need to figure all of this out before they do. I don't trust them. If they find the cross, they might not give it back for the Anniversary Celebration tomorrow. If they do give it back, the entire village will think they're heroes."

I couldn't imagine those guys looking like heroes. The mere thought of it nauseated me.

"Then let's get to work," I said, opening the library door.

Mrs. Pruit, who was sitting at the front desk, commented as soon as she saw us.

"Two days in a row, Angus and Maggie. How lucky for me! What brings you to the library so early in the morning? You kids are a little old for story time."

She looked me up and down suspiciously. "You're that new O'Hare boy who moved in on Brook Street," she concluded. "You were loitering around outside the church yesterday while the other kids were enjoying my Youth Group meeting."

"Um yes, that's me," I confirmed, staring at the ground. "I was waiting for Maggie and Angus."

"Mrs. Pruit, how do we find out the address of a former resident of Black Creek?" Angus asked, eager to divert her attention.

"Why do you want to know something like that? What are you kids up to?" she asked with a suspicious look.

Angus stammered, "I'm um, I'm writing an article about an older Black Creek family and I want to fact-check where they lived."

The three of us smiled at Mrs. Pruit and her eyes lit up.

"That's very interesting, Angus Fisher! I never took you for a journalist. I won't ask which family you're going to write about. I want to be surprised when I read it for myself. Follow me. I'll show you what to look for."

I pulled out my phone and texted Angus.

Me
Why not just ask her where Randall McPhee lived? Maybe she knows.

PING! Angus replied.

Angus
Cause she talks to my mom all the time. My mom will ask a million questions, and Donny will find out and tell Ricky.

"You boys put those phones on vibrate or turn them off!" Mrs. Pruit demanded.

We put our phones back in our pockets and she led us through the library, past the stacks of books and rows of study tables, to a section at the back. Two strange-looking computers sat on a table beside a tall oak cabinet with small drawers.

"This machine will read a microfiche. Do you kids know what a microfiche reader is?"

Angus, Maggie, and I exchanged confused glances and shrugged.

"Nope," Maggie said.

"Why, of course you don't," Mrs. Pruit said. "Sydney Raymond is the only child I know of that is aware of how to use these machines. With computers and tablets and the internet, most kids would have no reason to know about them now. A microfiche reader enlarges old records that have been shrunk onto a flat plastic card and stored to save space. It was used for newspapers, magazines, and town records."

"Here's one. She pulled a microfiche out of a cabinet drawer. "In Black Creek, we still use the microfiche for certain records, including old copies of the Black Creek Sun. Eventually, everything will get moved into a database, but for now, we're stuck with these. You take the plastic film and place it in the reader, like this." She demonstrated, placing the film under a flat piece of glass in the machine. "The magnified document comes up on the screen. You can scroll up and down using this knob. The town records are organized by year and separated by the type of record. See?"

"Cool," said Angus. "Thanks, Mrs. Pruit."

She nodded, took the microfiche back out, and placed it back in the cabinet.

"My advice is to start with the Black Creek telephone books. Black Creek only started making its own phone books in the 1980s. If you're looking for something listed before then, you may have to go to the Newbury city library."

"Thank you, Mr. Pruit," Angus said again.

"I'll leave you three to it. I have a group of little ones coming in at any moment. I expect you to keep quiet and not disturb my story time, and don't forget, Angus Fisher, I want to see that article when it's done."

Angus nodded, cursing under his breath after Mrs. Pruit walked away. While he sat down at a microfiche reader, Maggie and I started searching the cabinets. Maggie found the drawer housing the microfiche records from the 1990s. After a few minutes of flipping through the various dividers, she announced, "I've found the old phone books."

I moved to stand beside her as she went through the microfiches.

"Look, they're organized by year, like the town records," I observed. "Look for 1993 first since we know Randall McPhee died in 1994."

"Here it is," she said, pulling it out.

"Ssshhhhhh," warned Mrs. Pruit, turning away from the group of pre-school kids who had just arrived and were gathered around her.

Maggie ignored her and handed Angus a piece of plastic film, and he placed it into the reader. The image of a phone book came up on the screen. Angus started scrolling through the alphabetical list of names, looking for McPhee. We stood behind his chair, watching the screen closely.

"I can't believe I have to write an article about a Black Creek family, so I have something to show Mrs. Pruit! What was I thinking?" he whispered. Then he cried, "Found it!"

"Shhhhhh!" came from the front of the library.

He pointed to the screen. McPhee, R., 1133 County Road #3, Black Creek.

"That must be it," Angus said.

"Should we check it out?" I asked. "See if it's the property that's on the map?"

"Let's do it!" Angus whispered. "I know where that county road is, and I think I sort of know where that address would be. My dad took me fishing at a pond near there last summer. It's close enough that we can ride our bikes."

"But what if someone else lives there now?" Maggie asked.

"We can ask them if Randall McPhee ever lived there. Maybe they'll even let us look around," I said.

Maggie seemed doubtful. "Okay, I guess. Let's go," she said.

"Ssshhhhhhh!" Mrs. Pruit scowled at us.

Maggie and Angus hurried for the door. I followed behind, trying to hide my phone from Mrs. Pruit as I typed the address into my notes App. It wasn't until I was already outside that I realized we'd left the microfiche in the reader. Mrs. Pruit would be mad, but I was too excited to get to the farm to go back and put it away.

"Wait for me!" I said.

Chapter Twenty-six

We grabbed our bikes from the racks outside of the library. As I turned my bike around, I saw Ricky standing across the street, watching us.

I motioned to Maggie and Angus and pointed.

"Is Ricky following us now?"

"It's possible," Angus said. "He's nosing around for sure. It's not like he's a bookworm, and I doubt he's going to circle time!"

"Forget about him for now," Maggie said. "We have the address and he doesn't. Let's just go to the farm."

"Are you guys hungry?" Angus asked, buckling up his bike helmet. "It's almost 11."

"You're always hungry!" Maggie said, rolling her eyes.

"Let's go to my house first, before the farm," I said.

As we biked away, I looked back over my shoulder. Ricky was heading into the library. He was up to something, but I'd do what Maggie suggested and worry about him later.

Angus headed straight for my kitchen. He filled up water bottles from the water dispenser in the refrigerator, one for each of us.

"We don't have time to pack snacks, Angus," I said, spreading out the map on the kitchen island. "We should look at the map again."

Angus looked disappointed but found some granola bars, cookies and apples anyway and put them and the water into his backpack. He kept a granola bar aside, opened it, and shoved half the bar in his mouth.

"Let's look at this more closely to see if there are any clues we've missed," I suggested.

"Is there a marker on here that we didn't see the first time, like an odd-looking rock or something?" Maggie asked.

"No and there isn't even a scale or anything on the map. I guess we'll have to check out the property and start looking around," I said.

The front door slammed, and Janine and her friend Brittany walked into the living room. They were carrying smoothies from the Daily Ground.

"I can't believe that Rodney Bucci jerk stood you up like that and…" Brittany was saying until Janine raised her hand and cut her off mid-sentence.

"Hello, pukes," she said.

Brittany plopped herself down on the sofa while Janine came into the kitchen and headed toward the refrigerator.

I slid the map away and folded it nonchalantly, so it wouldn't draw her interest.

"What are the babies up to today?" Janine asked.

"Don't you two have some nails to polish and people to bad

mouth?" I asked.

"In case you've forgotten, I'm supposed to know what you and your zit-faced little friends are up to this afternoon," she said. "You know Marian expects me to watch out for you."

"We're not up to anything dangerous," I assured her. "Besides. I've told you before. I can text Mom myself."

"Fine, just be home before dinner. Don't forget, Marian is ordering Chinese food tonight and wants to watch a movie with us. You need to be back here before she gets home from work at 4. Come on, Brit." She and Brittany got up from the couch and the two of them headed upstairs.

"I forgot about dinner and the movie," I said. Maggie, Angus, and I exchanged worried looks.

"It's not a quick bike ride to the farm. I don't know exactly how long, but it's outside of town," Angus pointed out.

"We'll just try not to take too long, so I can get back from the farm on time. We have to go. The Anniversary Celebration starts tomorrow!"

PING!

"Guys, Sydney answered my question in her blog chat!" Angus said, showing us his phone.

Maggie and I gathered around and read Sydney's response.

> Hi Angus–Randall McPhee was a volunteer at the church and the caretaker of the Gilded Cross. What have you found out? I can use some help! I have a photo of Mr. McPhee that I found when my uncle let me go through some of his old photos. I'll send it to you.

The photo loaded and came into view frame by frame. Two men stood side by side, smiling, each holding a plate with a large piece of pie.

"I'd be smiling too if I had a piece of pie like that!" Angus said.

Maggie ignored him. "This is an old photo, but the guy on the left looks like Father Joe."

I examined the man on the right. He was at least a head taller than Father Joe and was wearing a white-collared shirt and jeans.

"The face looks very familiar," I said. "The man in the photo is younger than the old man that I keep seeing, but I'm pretty sure it's the same guy."

PING!

"Sydney sent another message," Angus said.

Angus – I hope you got the photo. Just so you know, when I investigated the missing cross, I asked my uncle what really happened the night of the break-in and who he thought tried to steal the Gilded Cross. He said Mr. McPhee recognized the two robbers. They were a couple of local teenagers and McPhee scared them off, but my uncle thinks they tried to find out where the cross was hidden. He suspects they confronted Mr. McPhee in the church office just before he collapsed and died. There was talk around the village that the teenagers were a couple of locals, Billy Tyler and Sonny Bucci. They were always getting into trouble. Nobody saw or could prove anything, so nothing was done about it.

"Look at those family names, Bucci and Tyler. They must be related to Rodney and Ricky!" Maggie said.

CHAPTER TWENTY-SEVEN

"So, we're right! Ricky is following us around," I said. "Maybe he and Rodney became curious about the cross when Sydney started blogging about it. Maybe they know about their family connection to the story. Now they're looking for it so they can give it back and be the heroes. After all of our hard work!"

"Or maybe they want to keep the cross and not give it back at all." Maggie said.

"Whatever their reason is for wanting it, I doubt it's a good one. We need to hurry up and figure out where the Gilded Cross is hiding before they do," Angus said.

"We'd better get moving," I added. I slid off my kitchen island stool and grabbed my backpack from the living room.

Angus picked up his backpack too, and we hurried out the door.

Angus was in the lead for our ride to the McPhee farm. Maggie followed and I was last in line. It turned out the ride was longer than I thought. Angus' long legs made pedaling look easier for him. I felt like I had to work twice as hard just to keep pace. We rode straight down Black Creek Road to the south side of the village. Just past the old mill and the abandoned toy factory, we turned left onto County Road 3, passing a house, a farm, and a wooded area.

We cycled for what seemed like a half hour past house numbers 1111, 1123, and finally we reached a rusty sign showing 1133. The sign dangled at an awkward angle from a crooked wooden post. Far back from the road at the end of a long driveway, lined by opposite rows of maple and oak trees, was a brown brick two-story farmhouse with a large red barn behind it.

Angus stopped pedaling, and Maggie and I did too.

"A long driveway, just like it shows on the map!" I said, breathing hard.

"This has to be it," Angus said.

We biked down the overgrown gravel driveway, the long grass brushing and scratching at my legs.

When I reached the end of the driveway, Maggie and Angus had already jumped off their bikes. I lay my bike down on the grass with theirs, adjusted my backpack, and hurried across the front yard toward the weather-beaten farmhouse. The house had a black front door, black shutters, and a small covered front porch. It was clearly abandoned but looked to be in relatively good condition.

"If it weren't for the peeling paint on the door and the two broken windows on the first floor, you'd think someone stills lives here," I said.

"I hope no one's here now." Maggie said.

I retrieved the map from my pocket.

“Look! The house is in the same spot as the building on the map, just to the right of the driveway,” I said, pointing to the location it on the paper. “The Xs end in the middle the area behind the house, and hopefully that’s where we’ll find the cross, but I think we should also go inside and see if there’s anything that tells us for sure that Randall McPhee lived here.”

“Maybe we should split up,” Maggie said. “One of us can go in. The other two can check the back of the house where the X’s stop.”

“Good idea,” I said. “You and Angus can check the back, and I’ll look around the house.”

“But I want to test out my App in the house!” Angus protested. “What if it’s haunted?”

“Are you okay if both Angus and I check out the house, Maggie?” I asked. “Or do you want me to come with you?”

“Nope. I’ll yell if I have a problem. I’ll find you guys when I’m done.”

“Alright. Let’s do this,” I said. “Since you’re looking outside, Maggie, you take the map.”

I handed the map to her and she headed around the side of the house toward the backyard. I stepped up onto the steps of the greying porch, moving carefully, testing the wooden boards to make sure that the floor could support my weight. Once I was sure it was safe, I motioned for Angus to follow.

Angus pulled out his phone.

“The reception isn’t great. Hopefully, my App will still kick in but it should work without it.”

He held his phone in the air and pointed it at the house, before joining me on the porch.

The screen door squealed in protest as I opened it. I knocked on the front door.

"Why are you knocking?"

"It's the polite thing to do," I said, with a shrug.

Angus looked at me, confused. "But nobody lives here."

"You never know. We could warn the ghost we're coming in!" I chuckled.

I turned the doorknob. "It's unlocked."

I pushed the door open and walked inside.

CHAPTER TWENTY-EIGHT

Angus followed me into foyer of the farmhouse, still holding his phone in the air.

I paused to let my eyes adjust to the darker interior. A long hallway stretched out in front of us with a staircase against the wall to the right. On the left was a doorway into the living room. I led the way.

The room was empty except for a single wooden rocking chair in the front corner of the room beside the window as if waiting for someone to sit there. Sunlight poured in through the front windows, illuminating the dust hanging in the air, creating a light, hazy fog in the room. The walls were covered with white flowered, wallpaper.

We walked through the living room and under an archway into the empty dining room with the same flowery wallpaper.

Angus walked over to examine the faded photos hanging on one of the walls.

"Look at this," he said. He peered closely at it. "Do you think one of these men is Randall McPhee?"

I joined him to have a look. The photo was of a family, possibly at a reunion. Six people were gathered in a group outdoors under a large tree, maybe one of the trees we passed beside the driveway. An old man and an old woman sat side by side in lawn chairs with four adults standing behind them.

"Look at the older man on the far left." Angus pointed. "He looks a bit like the man in the photo Sydney sent us."

I instantly recognized him.

"That's him! The ghost. That's the man that I've been seeing. It's Randall McPhee. This must be his property!"

"Then we know we're in the right place," Angus concluded.

I walked through the dining room into the kitchen. It was still in good shape except for a couple of the green cupboard doors that had broken hinges. The walls were painted a dusty rose color and were bare other than a hanging calendar dated February, 1994. A door at the rear of the kitchen led straight to the backyard.

I felt uncomfortable being there, like I was intruding into someone's life. But I reminded myself, it was Randall McPhee who had reached out to me! He wanted me there.

I leaned over a deep white sink, stained with rusty streaks, and rubbed at the dirty window above it. The red barn in the distance came into view.

Someone stood just outside of the barn door. Was that Maggie?

I rubbed harder on the window. It definitely wasn't Maggie. Who was that?

"Angus!" I called, and I leaned forward, my nose almost touching the glass, the sink digging into my stomach. The figure was wearing a familiar plaid shirt, overalls, and black rubber boots. It was Randall McPhee!

CHAPTER TWENTY-NINE

"Angus!" I called again, my eyes fixed on McPhee.

Then McPhee looked right at me, lifted his arm and motioned to me to follow him. He walked to the barn door, stopped, and disappeared. And for the first time, I wasn't afraid. Seeing the ghost was like seeing someone I knew.

Angus hurried into the kitchen and joined me at the window.

"What is it? What are you looking at?" he asked.

"Randall McPhee is outside," I said. "I just saw him out the window."

Angus glanced out the window, canvassing the backyard.

"I don't see anything!" He started pointing and waving his phone in the air. "Nothing. Where is he?"

Just then Maggie burst in through the back door, map in hand. "Guys," she said, spreading open the map on the dusty wooden counter beside the sink. "I've been following the Xs, and it looks like they lead to the barn which is strange because the barn isn't drawn on the map."

She pointed to the final X. "I think the cross must be hidden in the barn."

"I think you're right!" I said. "I just saw the ghost of Randall McPhee again, and he signaled to me. I think he wants us to go into the barn."

"I want to see the ghost!" Angus complained.

"I'm not afraid of him anymore," I declared. "He just wants our help."

"I'm not scared, because I don't think I'll see the ghost anyway," Angus said, "but you never know. I sure hope I do, and the barn may be where it finally happens."

"We need to find out what's in that barn," I said, heading for the back door.

"Then let's go!" Maggie said, following close behind.

We walked to the front of the barn, through the tall grass, past an abandoned hay wagon and a rusty tractor.

"I'll get the door," said Angus, but when he tried to open the large wooden sliding door, it didn't move. It only gave in when all three of us pulled on it at the same time.

We stepped into a large room with scattered hay and chunks of dirt, possibly dried up old manure on the floor. It had a few stalls for horses and a ladder leading up to a large loft over the stalls. Other than a few pieces of farming equipment and a light blue dresser shoved against the rear wall, the barn looked empty. The small windows were cracked or had lost sections of their glass panes. The outdoor breeze whistled eerily as it blew though the open spaces.

"I'll take the loft," Maggie said. She climbed up the ladder and disappeared from sight. A moment later, she shouted down, "There's nothing up here!"

Angus and I checked the stalls. Nothing.

"There has to be something for us to find in this barn!" I said, as Maggie came down the ladder.

"Let's look in the dresser," Angus said, and he and I headed to the back of the barn.

BEEP! BEEP! BEEP! BEEP!
BEEP! BEEP! BEEP! BEEP!

The noise from Angus' phone screamed at us. I jumped.

The screen on his phone turned a bright pink.

"My App is picking something up! It's working!"

Maggie looked at Angus in disbelief.

Out of nowhere, the breeze changed into strong wind. It howled through the windows, swirling the hay all around the floor at our feet. The room became frigidly cold almost instantly. We could see our breath in the frosty air.

"That's strange." Maggie said, rubbing her arms. "It's not cold outside at all. What's going on?"

Finally, it clicked for her. "Is something paranormal happening? Angus, that App might actually work!"

The wind had pushed away the hay that covered the floor around the dresser. It looked like the hay had been hiding something. I knelt on the floor and swept away the remaining pieces with my hands.

"Look!" I said. "I think this might be a trap door! Help me move the dresser."

Maggie and Angus lent a hand, and with the dresser out of the way, I felt around the edges of the trapdoor. A rope was tucked underneath one corner. I grabbed it and pulled. The hatch lifted easily, exposing a small crawlspace. Five steep wooden steps led down to the dark room.

"We've come this far. We can't stop now," I said. "I'm going down there."

"Me too, but it's so dark," Maggie said. "How are we going to see anything?"

"Let's use our phones," Angus said.

Maggie and Angus pulled their phones out of their pockets and activated their flashlights. It was enough light for them to lead the way, so I left my phone in my pocket and followed them down the steps.

Once at the bottom, Maggie's head and mine were inches from the ceiling. Angus' head almost touched it. The smell of mothballs filled my nostrils and my eyes watered. Why did people use those things?

The combined light from Maggie and Angus' phones illuminated the empty dirt floor.

"It wouldn't be easy for an adult to move around in here," I observed. "Anything put in this crawlspace was meant to be stored away for a long time, or hidden."

But there was nothing down here, nothing but thick grey cobwebs all over the corners of walls. My heart sank.

I turned and was about to make my way up the steps to look somewhere else when Maggie cried out,

"Look! There's something under the stairs. I can hardly see it, but it's there!"

We crawled under the stairs and found an old wooden trunk. Angus and I pulled it out from its hiding place. It had a metal clip on each side at the front and a large keyhole in the middle. I opened the metal clips and tried to lift the trunk lid. It was locked. Randall McPhee sure was good at locking things up! Maybe that's why Father Joe had asked him to hide the cross.

"Hey, Jamie! Did you bring the keys you found in the church tower?" Maggie asked.

"Good idea. I almost forgot!"

I had been carrying the keys around with me in my pocket ever since that night in the church tower, just in case we needed them.

"That must be what this big, funny looking key is for," I said. I inserted the long metal shaft into the trunk's keyhole and turned it. It fit! It was stiff at first, but after a few attempts - click!

I lifted the heavy lid.

Chapter Thirty

Maggie and Angus shone their lights into the trunk while I held up the lid. We peered inside. It looked full, but with what? Old, yellowing newspapers were strewn across the top.

Angus took over holding up the lid while I pulled out the newspapers and dropped them in a pile on the dirt floor. Maggie picked up one of sheets.

"It's dated February 25th, 1994," she read. "This has to be the hiding place! That's around the same time as the articles that Sydney posted."

The remaining top half of the trunk was filled with clothes and books. In the bottom half were a few old photo albums, stacked on top of one another.

"There's something under those albums," Angus said.

"I think you're right Angus." I took the albums out and placed them on the newspapers.

At the bottom of the trunk lay a long flat box with a gold top and a white bottom. I lifted it out and held it, letting it rest along on the length of my forearm. I slid the lid off with my other hand, then unfolded layer after layer of white tissue paper. Angus and Maggie looked on, holding their phones steady.

The gemstones encased in the Gilded Cross sparkled in the light of the phones.

I was stunned. "Wow! It's the most beautiful thing I've ever seen!"

A large ruby surrounded by diamonds sat in the centre of the cross. Rows of small emeralds led to another diamond - encircled ruby at each of the four tips.

"It's the Gilded Cross! We've finally found it!" Maggie said. "We can return it in time for the Church Anniversary Celebration tomorrow."

"It looks like something you'd find in a pirate's treasure chest," Angus said.

"Well, well, well!" A voice called from the top of the stairs. "What do we have here?"

Startled, I almost dropped the cross.

Maggie, Angus, and I looked up at the top of the steps. It was Rodney Bucci!

He was standing on the barn floor, arms crossed, looking down at us through the trapdoor opening.

"Me and Ricky knew that you nerds were up to something, sneaking around the church, researching in the library. Too bad you weren't smart enough to cover your tracks."

I lowered the cross out of sight beside the trunk and managed to slide it into my backpack before the three of us stood up to face Rodney. I silently cursed myself for leaving that microfiche in the machine at the library. That must be how Rodney found us.

"Get lost, Rodney!" Angus cried. "You have nothing to do with this. We're the ones who've figured it all out!"

I had never seen Angus so angry.

"Boo-hoo!" Rodney said, pretending to wipe away tears. "I guess life just ain't fair! Ricky's dad and my dad were blamed for trying to take that thing. I'm going to return it and make my family the village heroes. Now get up here and hand over the cross!" He held out his hand.

After everything that we had gone through, I wasn't about to give up without a fight.

"You'll have to come and get it yourself!" I yelled.

Randall McPhee wanted us to find the cross, not him. There was no way I was turning it over to Rodney. I didn't trust him.

"Then I guess I'm busting heads!" Rodney threatened.

Maggie's back straightened. Her hands clenched in fists. "Get ready to fight all three of us then!"

"All right," Rodney said. "It's your funeral."

Rodney took two steps down the short staircase and suddenly, he toppled forward, right over the bottom three steps, landing on his side on the dirt floor. Maggie, Angus, and I had to jump out of the way to avoid being knocked over.

"What happened?" I asked. I looked up, searching for an explanation.

"Hey there, puke-face."

Janine was standing at the top of the stairs!

CHAPTER THIRTY-ONE

"What are you doing here?" I asked.

I was shocked to see my sister, and even more shocked that she was helping us! It was almost too much to take in at once.

"Never mind that! Hurry and get up here, fast, all three of you," she ordered.

Rodney was scrambling around on the ground, stirring up dust. He looked up and saw Janine.

"What the…?" he asked, dazed.

Realizing we only had seconds to get out of there, Maggie side-stepped Rodney and ran up the steps first, followed by Angus. I was right behind them, backpack on, with only two steps to go when Rodney grabbed my ankle. I kicked my leg, trying to dislodge my foot from his grip. Janine took hold of my arm. I guess she had scooped up old dried up manure in her other hand, because she threw a chunk of something at Rodney. The manure hit him right in the face and broke apart on impact. He let go of my ankle to use both hands to wipe the dirt out of his eyes, and that gave Janine just enough time to help me scramble up onto the barn floor.

Janine slammed the trapdoor closed. "You'll think again before you ever stand up another girl, Rodney Bucci! Now, all of you, help me move the dresser before he tries to get out."

The four of us pushed the blue dresser back over the trapdoor.

Rodney screamed and banged on the door. "Let me out of here! I'll make you pay!"

"No, you won't," Janine called back, "or everyone will know that you got your butt kicked by a girl!"

Janine turned to us again. "Now, let's get out of here. That creepy Ricky Tyler is lurking around in the house. He'll be out here any minute and let Rodney out."

We hurried after Janine to the barn door but stopped when she held up her hand. She peeked outside.

"The coast is clear. I think that jerk is still in the house."

We darted out behind her, ran across the back of the property to the treed driveway, and sprinted to our bikes. Janine had parked her bike with ours. We hopped on and then stopped to catch our breath.

"How did you know we were here?" I asked her.

Janine pushed her kickstand back. "Kendra heard those idiots talking about finding you guys. They stopped talking when they saw her, so she didn't hear why they wanted to find you. She knows I'm supposed to look out for you, so she texted me to warn me. I went downstairs, but you must have just left. I jumped on my bike to go and look for you, and I saw the three of you riding out of the village on Black Creek Road. While I was riding home, I saw Rodney and Ricky following you on their bikes. I stopped to text and call you to warn you. When you didn't answer, I figured you were still riding your bike so I decided to follow Rodney and Ricky."

"I didn't see the call or get the text. I haven't looked at my phone since we got here, but thanks, Janine. You got here just in time!"

I couldn't believe Janine cared about me enough that she followed Rodney and Ricky all the way to the farm.

"Thank you!" Maggie and Angus said in unison.

"You can thank me later. We need to get out of here now! By the way, this doesn't mean that I like you little pukes."

The ride back to the village seemed much longer than the ride to the farm. I kept looking over my shoulder, worried that we were being followed. I was flooded with relief when the four of us arrived at my house and I saw Mom's minivan. Rodney and Ricky wouldn't bother us, at least for the time being if they saw our van in the driveway and thought Mom might be home.

"Hi, kids," Mom called down from upstairs as we all trooped inside.

"Hi, Marian," Janine said. Then she glared at the three of us."You have thirty seconds to tell me what's going on or I'm upstairs telling Mom where I found you."

Chapter Thirty-Two

"Okay, okay," I said.

We went into the kitchen, and I launched into the story. Maggie and Angus filled in some details along the way. I paused briefly before mentioning my visions, bracing myself for Janine's nasty comments, but when I described them, Janine was shockingly silent. Maybe she had changed.

When I got to the part about the barn and finding the trunk, I gently removed the Gilded Cross out of my backpack and showed it to her. Her jaw dropped, and for once she was stunned into silence.

"I knew you had some 'out there' abilities, but they led you to find the Gilded Cross? This cross is priceless! What are you going to do with it?"

"We're not going to keep it," I said. "We're planning to return it to the church for the Anniversary Celebration tomorrow."

Maggie nodded. "We have to get it back to the church right away! Those meatheads want to get their hands on it and probably have their entire gang involved by now."

Janine's face lit up. "Can I help you with that? Let me go with you to the church. I can fend off those goons, and I can help explain what happened."

"I suppose we need all the help we can get," I said. I was a bit hesitant, still surprised by this new 'nice' Janine, but we needed her help.

"Mom," Janine shouted. "We're going out. We'll be back before dinner in an hour."

Mom called back from upstairs. "Okay. Make sure you come back soon. I'm ordering Chinese food."

We headed back out on our bikes but hadn't gone far when Maggie yelled, "Look," and pointed behind us.

Rodney and Ricky rounded the corner of the crescent. They hadn't spotted us yet. We started pedaling faster to get ahead of them.

I was riding beside Janine.

"I don't think we can beat them to the church. They're pretty close behind," I said.

Janine nodded in agreement. "If they see us, we won't make it. Ricky is an athlete and he and Rodney could have friends waiting at the church. One text from Rodney and they all jump. We have to throw them off our trail."

Janine had gotten us this far, so we all followed without protest.

We kept riding as fast as we could, but at the end of our street, Janine jumped off her bike and parked it on its kickstand in the front yard of a little grey brick bungalow.

"This is Kendra's house," she told us. "Come on, guys. Get off your bikes."

"We don't have time to visit Kendra!" I cried.

"I know that! We're not going inside," Janine said.

"Then why are we leaving our bikes?" Maggie asked.

"Rodney and Ricky will recognize my bike and see three other bikes and think we're hiding out here instead of going to the church," Janine said. "This could buy us some time. Maybe they'll stake out Kendra's while we head off on foot. Anyway, let's lose them first and then figure out what to do. Come on. Follow me."

Maggie, Angus, and I dropped our bikes and let Janine hurry us straight across Black Creek Road, sticking to the treed side of the street.

Janine took a sharp right and led us down to another large crescent.

"Let's find a backyard to hide in for now," she said.

We approached an overgrown yellow-sided bungalow in the middle of the crescent. It stood out from the other properties because it had knee-high grass and wild unruly shrubs covering the bottom half of a large front window.

"Let's try hiding behind this place," I said when the side door swung open.

"In here!" a girl called out to us. "Quick! Those guys just turned onto the street."

"Sydney?" Angus asked.

CHAPTER THIRTY-THREE

Janine grabbed my arm and pulled me toward the side of the house. Maggie and Angus followed.

We stepped inside and found ourselves in a small mudroom. Stairs against the side wall led to the basement.

"Downstairs," Sydney ordered. I was happy to comply. We all dutifully followed Sydney to her basement.

Basements in most homes have a sofa, posters on the walls, a TV, even a ping pong or pool table and a beer fridge. Not this one. This room looked like a command center. Four monitors were mounted side by side on the back wall above a long desk with a laptop and a large computer screen. The side wall was a giant whiteboard with newspaper articles, photos, and handwritten notes scattered over it, all held up by magnets. Sydney covered the lone window in the room in a black sheet.

I studied the first monitor. It displayed an image of the side yard and the driveway outside Sydney's house and then switched to the backyard of the house. The second monitor panned back and forth, showing views of the crescent and each entrance.

Wow! Sydney must have installed cameras on the street-lights. The third monitor had a clear view of her street out front. I could see Rodney and Ricky biking past, looking for us. We had just escaped in time. They clearly had no idea we were there and rode right by Sydney's house. The fourth monitor showed a view of the sky, which was clear.

Angus was in awe. "What is this place?" he asked.

"I know! It looks bad!" Sydney said. "I swear, I'm not spying on my neighbors."

"Are you kidding? This is my dream basement!" Angus said, his gaze shifting from monitor to monitor.

"I think I know why those guys are chasing you," Sydney said. "You've found the Gilded Cross, haven't you?"

"How did you know?" I asked. Sydney looked a lot like I remembered from the first time I met her, but today an orange bandana covered her hair, and she was wearing a black t-shirt with a picture of an brown alien's head. The large alien eyes were made of silver sequins. It felt like both the alien's eyes and Sydney's were fixed on our faces.

"I figured from Angus' message that you guys were looking for the cross and I made a guess. Why else would those buffoons be following you?" Sydney said. "I only wish you had let me know what you were doing. I would have helped you."

"Everything happened so fast!" I said. "We've only been searching for a few days, and with Rodney and Ricky following us around, we had to act fast."

"I was going to answer you, I swear!" Angus reassured her.

"That's fine. I get it," Sydney said.

I exchanged looks with Maggie, Angus, and Janine. Angus was the first to speak. He told Sydney about my visions, but before he'd said more than a few words, Maggie shot him a dirty look.

"What's wrong?" he asked. "Sydney writes about stuff like this all of the time. I think she'll believe us more than anyone else would! Jamie, do you want to tell her?"

I sighed. "Okay, here goes."

When I finished my story, I saw Angus was right. Sydney didn't look a bit shocked.

"Can I write an article for my blog about this?" she asked. "This is so cool!"

"First things first, children!" Janine said. "There's no happy ending just yet. We still have to return the cross to the church."

"Janine is right. I spoke too soon," Sydney said.

"You should know that after I sent you that last message, I asked my uncle about Randall McPhee again about the robbery. He told me he remembers Randall complaining that Ricky and Rodney's dads were stalking him."

"So they did try to steal the cross!" Maggie said.

"It looks that way," Sydney said. "You can't trust Rodney and Ricky. Who knows what their plans are if they get their hands on the cross."

"I'll bet they have the rest of their gang involved by now," Maggie added.

"They'll stop us from getting anywhere near the church," Janine said.

"Well, we ditched our bikes, so we'll have to get to there on foot. But how do we do it and avoid them?" I asked.

"And even if we got it there, who exactly would we give it

to? And how do we explain how we found it? Ghosts helping us? If Mrs. Pruit was there and overheard, imagine the stories that would be spread around the village!" Angus said.

"Do you guys trust me enough to leave the Gilded Cross with me?" Sydney asked.

"Why would we do that?" Janine asked.

"Because Rodney, Ricky, and their gang aren't looking for me," Sydney said. "Plus, my uncle is the priest, remember? I can slip into his residence beside the church anytime I want, and it won't look suspicious if anyone sees me. The rest of you can distract Rodney, Ricky, and whoever else they've rounded up for help."

"I guess that's not a bad idea, but why don't you just text your uncle and ask him to come here and get the cross now?" Janine asked. "We could give it to him ourselves that way."

"That would make sense, but he's out of town and won't be back until tomorrow morning, right before the Anniversary Celebration starts," Sydney said.

"But if you take the cross to the residence now and leave it overnight, and your uncle's not there, what happens if Rodney and Ricky figure out what you've done? What if they break in there to look for it?" Janine asked.

"Another priest is visiting. I'll ask him to lock it in the church safe, and hopefully he won't ask many questions. Happy now?"

Janine looked satisfied with that and glanced over at us to see if we agreed.

"Yes, but if we return the cross now, how do we distract Rodney, Ricky, and their friends?" I asked.

Sydney motioned us to gather around her as she sat down at her computer and opened a map of Black Creek. She zoomed in on her street and brought the map up on one of the larger monitors so we could all see it easily.

"Look. There are three separate routes from here to the church, a path on the other end of my crescent from where you came in and another one next door to my house. Both paths end at the park, and then you can cut through the park to get to the church. The third route leads back to Black Creek Road and you can walk straight to the church from there. You four can split up into pairs. Maggie and Angus can take the path at the end of the street. Jamie and Janine can take the path next door. I'll take Black Creek Road."

"Ok," I said. "And if Rodney, Ricky or any of their friends chase us, we'll lead them away from the church and Father Joe's residence."

Maggie, Angus, and Janine nodded in agreement.

I pulled the cross out of my backpack. It sparkled in the light from the monitors and computer screens as I handed it to Sydney.

CHAPTER THIRTY-FOUR

We stood at the side of Sydney's house to get organized. Sydney repeated the plan, so we were all clear.

"Everyone has their phones?" she asked, pulling hers out of the pocket of her jean shorts.

We each grabbed our phones to show her.

"Okay, let's set up a group text," Sydney said.

I volunteered to do it and entered everyone's numbers into my phone, then sent a test message. All of the phones chimed.

"Now, let's do this!" Sydney said.

Maggie and Angus headed to the end of the crescent. Janine and I turned down the path beside Sydney's house. Meanwhile, Sydney walked up her crescent toward Black Creek Road, the cross hidden in a large cross-body canvas bag. Angus and I still had our backpacks with us which were useful decoys.

Janine and I started up the path, staying on the lookout for

Rodney or Ricky. I texted the others.

Me
All clear so far.

PING! PING!

Maggie
Same here.

PING! PING!

Sydney
Here too.

Janine and I walked along our path until it reached the street behind Sydney's. The path continued on the other side. Janine looked to her left, and I looked to my right.

"I don't see anyone. Do you?" Janine asked.

"Nope."

We hurried across the road and headed down the path.

PING! PING!

Sydney
I'm on Black Creek Road. I see some kids standing by the church.

Sydney
Not Rodney and Ricky but it looks like a couple of their friends. I'll go into the library just in case they stop me.

Maggie
We're almost at the park.

Me
So are we.

Both the paths ended at the top of the grass that surrounded the playground at the front of the park. As we reached the grass, I saw Maggie and Angus emerge from their path. The church was visible in the distance, and a group of men were setting up party tents on the grounds beside it, preparing for the celebration the next day. To their right was an unobstructed view of Mervin's General Store and the Daily Ground.

I spotted Rodney and Ricky, sitting on a park bench not fifty feet from us, their bikes leaning on the back of the bench.

Janine and I froze. So did Maggie and Angus.

Ricky and Rodney were looking at their phones and didn't seem to notice us or them.

I typed as fast as I could.

Me
There they are! Let's distract them! We'll make them follow us!

PING! PING! PING!

The chimes from our phones were loud enough to catch Ricky's attention. He looked up, saw us, and nudged Rodney, who also looked up.

"Get them!" Rodney shouted.

CHAPTER THIRTY-FIVE

"Come on. Let's go!" said Janine as Rodney started jogging toward us.

Ricky ran in Maggie and Angus's direction. Thankfully, neither guy thought to grab his bike to chase us.

"It's working! Rodney is right behind us!" I said.

"We'll lead him to our house. He won't bug us there," Janine said. We were approaching the edge of the park by the sidewalk. "We have a head start, but we have to keep moving."

We crossed the street together at a jog.

"Let's take the path just past the Daily Ground," I said.

We reached the path and started running. But Rodney was catching up.

"I don't think there's any way he can catch us, but when we get to the end of the path, turn on the jets," Janine said.

When we reached the edge of the path, we took a sharp left toward our house. Rodney, just at the beginning of the path, was still running after us. Janine was right. We were faster than Rodney, whose muscular bulk slowed him down.

Janine and I easily made it to the front door and inside before he came close to us.

I sat down on the couch to catch my breath. Janine went straight to the kitchen to get us each a glass of water. Mom called down to us from upstairs.

"Hi Marian!" Janine said.

PING! PING!

Janine and I checked our phones.

Maggie
Ricky caught up with us. He searched Angus' backpack but only found empty water bottles, granola bar wrappers and gross apple cores. After that he kept asking where the cross was. We told him they're too late, and he left us alone.

I laughed picturing Ricky digging his hands into Angus' backpack and ending up with dirty, slimy apple cores. I texted Maggie back.

Me
We made it to my house!

Just then, Sydney sent us an update.

Sydney
I made it! I cut through the library so Rodney and Ricky's friends wouldn't suspect anything. I went out the back door and walked through the back of the parking lot, crossed the park where all the people are setting up and made it to the residence. All good!

Janine and I exchanged looks of relief. I replied to Sydney for both of us.

Maggie chimed in immediately after.

The plan worked and the Gilded Cross had been safely returned to the church where it belonged.

Chapter Thirty-six

I woke up that Saturday morning, the morning of the Church Anniversary Celebration, to the sound of a commotion downstairs and a very familiar voice.

"Now don't be fussing over me, Marian," Grandma said. "I can look after myself. Don't you be late for work!"

I found Grandma in the front hall with her bags at her feet, smoothing her hair.

"There's my gorgeous grandson," she said, pulling me in to give me a big bear hug. The familiar scent of her perfume instantly comforted me.

"Your mother has just left to sell all of the houses in town!" she proclaimed.

Janine appeared in the foyer and grabbed one of Grandma's bags.

"Drop that bag and get over here," Grandma said. "You're not too old for a hug. And don't think for a minute you'll be calling me by my first name, young lady!"

"I won't, Grandma."

"Will you two show me around your new home?"

I was the first to reply. "I will!"

"I'll catch up with you, Grandma. I'm going to have a shower," Janine said.

I showed Grandma the house, room by room, and then brought her back to the kitchen. She insisted on making me some toast, then poured herself a cup of tea from the pot Mom had made earlier. She sat beside me at the table.

"Now then, I've been worried about you ever since our conversation last Christmas." Grandma reached out and grabbed my hand. "How have you been? Are you sleeping okay? Has that special sight of yours been bothering you? We don't have to talk about it if you're not comfortable."

"Well, that second sight was giving me some trouble when we first moved here," I began.

I told her all about the first weeks in Black Creek with the nightmares and the visions, meeting Maggie and Angus, the mystery of the missing Gilded Cross, and finally finding the cross in time for the Church Anniversary Celebration. That was more than I'd said to Mom! I told Grandma about how Janine helped me. Mom was surprised when I told her, but Grandma didn't seem to be.

"Your sister has a big heart even if she doesn't show it sometimes," Grandma said.

She continued, "You know, Jamie, your Grandpa Cornelius also had nightmares sometimes."

Grandma stopped and took a sip of her tea. "I didn't tell you everything at Christmas because I didn't want to tell you more than you could handle. One time, he had a dream with a message from a woman about a car accident and was able to pass it along to the woman's daughter. The daughter started changing her usual driving routes. He may have helped her avoid a major accident that happened on the interstate a few weeks later."

"Wow, really?" I was fascinated.

"Yes, indeed. Another time he received a message in a dream from a young boy to be given to his father. The man had just lost his son to cancer. Your Grandpa comforted the boy's father by telling him the boy was happy and safe."

"That's so awesome!" I said.

"Just know that the special sight may come at a cost, Dear, and that cost is the scary stuff that sometimes can't be explained. That part, you learn to live with."

Our conversation was interrupted by the pinging of my phone. It was Angus.

Angus
Check out the SydyBlog. You'll love it!

I opened the blog on my phone and read aloud.

The Gilded Cross is a large Spanish-style solid gold cross with diamonds, rubies, and emeralds. The cross had been missing after a robbery attempt forced Father Joseph Raymond to entrust local church volunteer Randall McPhee with its temporary safekeeping. McPhee, who interrupted the robbery, died unexpectedly shortly after taking charge of the cross, having never revealed its location.

The kids, Jamie O'Hare, Angus Fischer, and Maggie Zhou, investigated the mystery of the missing cross. They were looking around Randall McPhee's farm when they found the cross hidden away in a crawlspace under the barn. This is fantastic news for St. Bartholomew and the community of Black Creek! They have a piece of their history back. The Gilded Cross will be kept in a safety deposit box and a replica will be made. The church will only bring out the real thing for very important church and community celebrations.
A special mention to Janine O'Hare who helped the kids return the cross safely.

"I'm so proud of you, Jamie," Grandma said.

I texted Angus back.

Me
This is great news!

Sydney mentioned nothing about the ghost. She was cool! We'd have to keep hanging out with her.

Angus
I know, right?

Maggie
Just saw Sydney's post. Did you see it?

I made a group chat for the three of us.

Me
Yep! Awesome! Meet you guys at the Anniversary Celebration?

Angus
Yep. I'm leaving soon.

Maggie
Me too.

Me
See you there.

"Go and see your friends," Grandma said. "I'll come along to the Celebration later. I'll unpack here first and change my clothes."

CHAPTER THIRTY-SEVEN

Maggie and I were closing in on second place in the potato sack race at the park. We were a few feet from the finish line when I felt her weight knock me over, pushing us toward the finish. We won a ribbon for third place! And I thought I wasn't an athlete.

The Church Anniversary Celebration was turning out to be a big success. It looked like most of the villagers were there. The park was set up with activities like face-painting, a dunk tank, and a bouncy castle. The potato sack race was the last race of the morning after the egg-and-spoon race. Angus had been in that race and came in fifth place. To celebrate, he was doing one of his favorite things, eating. We found him sitting with Sydney at one of the picnic tables under the huge white party tent, enjoying a hot dog and a hamburger. Maggie and I grabbed a hot dog each and joined him. Mom had finished up work for the day and she and Grandma sat down with us, lunch plates in hand.

Sydney and Angus were speculating about who in the village might be an alien. Mrs. Pruit was at the top of Angus' list. Sydney also explained her theory that a sea monster lived in Black Creek Lake and showed us internet videos to prove it.

"Sydney, we should make our own horror movie together," Maggie said.

Sydney immediately perked up. "That would be fun!"

"I have no clue where I'll get the time to help with that," Angus said. "I have to write an article for Mrs. Pruit, remember? Maybe I'll write about finding the cross. She'd like that!"

"She sure would!" Maggie said. We all laughed.

Janine approached the table, probably on her way to meet her friends seated at the back.

"Hey, Grandma. How's it going, pukes?"

I knew nice Janine wouldn't last! Grandma shot Janine a look that meant "cut it out."

"Where's your boyfriend Rodney, or is it Ricky now?" I asked in retaliation.

"They won't be bothering any of us anymore, and that means the three of you, and Sydney, and all of my friends. I told them my friends and I would make sure they never get a date for the rest of their high school careers if they dare give us trouble again. If they say or do anything, they won't be getting a date for years!"

It was odd that Janine's mean girl tactics were being used to do the right thing, but I wasn't about to complain. I doubted she'd get any argument from Maggie, Angus or Sydney either.

"Works for us," Maggie said.

"Yeah, thanks," Angus said.

Sydney gave a thumbs up.

“Stay out of trouble, infants. I’m tired of babysitting you!” Janine said and walked away.

“Kids, pay attention,” Grandma said. She pointed at Father Joe, who had grabbed a mic at the front of the tent.

“Attention! Attention!”

The mic screeched and silenced the chattering crowd of people sitting at picnic tables and standing at the back. Father Joe seized the moment and started.

“I’d like to take a moment and thank all of you for coming today. St. Bartholomew has been a symbol of both the long history and continuity of our community. I’m grateful to have been a part of that for thirty years, but it’s each of you that keeps this community and parish going, and that’s what today is all about.”

Loud applause interrupted his speech. A few people whistled. The clapping faded and Father Joe continued.

“As you may have heard, one of St. Bartholomew’s most precious items, a gift given to the Parish at its opening one hundred and fifty years ago, the Gilded Cross, was missing for over twenty-five years but was located by a few inquisitive local children. The heroes found the cross and returned it to the church just yesterday. The cross will appear at mass tomorrow, so I hope all of you will join me. Please stand up Jamie O’Hare, Janine O’Hare, Angus Fisher, Maggie Zhou, and my niece, Sydney Raymond.”

Grandma looked at us and nodded, prompting us to comply.

Maggie, Angus, Sydney, and I looked at one another and stood up. Janine, sitting at a picnic table at the back, also stood up. Everyone in the crowd clapped and cheered. I felt very proud. I noticed Sydney’s face and neck flushed red. I guessed she didn’t enjoy being the center of attention.

When the applause ended, and people went back to their food and activities, Sydney stood up.

“I have to get back to my latest investigation,” she said.

She walked away before we could ask questions.

“You three should get ice cream, on me,” Grandma said. “You deserve it! Jamie, I’ll see you at home later.”

She reached into her purse and handed me the money.

“Thank you, Grandma!”

“Thanks! I’ve never said no to ice cream,” Angus said

“And you never will!” Maggie said.

Chapter Thirty-Eight

As Maggie, Angus, and I walked down Black Creek Road, enjoying our ice cream cones, I remembered my first day in Black Creek when Maggie took me on a tour. It was only a month ago, but I felt like I'd lived there forever. I had new friends, my sister was being kind of nice to me, and I wasn't afraid of my second sight. I could use it to help people. On top of all that, Randall McPhee could rest easy now that the Gilded Cross was found.

"This has been an amazing summer! I can't believe we go to school on Tuesday," I said. "I hated being the new kid when I first moved here, but now I'm excited to start. So, what are we going to do for the rest of the long weekend?"

"How about relax?" Maggie asked. "I'm still tired from the past week!"

We walked by the church and I held my breath, preparing for the feeling of eyes on the back of my head. Nothing.

I nudged Maggie. “I didn’t feel anything that time. Did you?”

“No, I didn’t!” Maggie said with a grin. “We can finally walk by the church in peace.”

“I wonder if I’ll still keep seeing and hearing stuff,” I said.

“I hope so. I think It’s the coolest thing ever,” Angus said. “People like you can make millions of dollars!”

Maggie’s glared disapprovingly at Angus. “It’s not all about the money, Angus.”

Angus defended himself. “I’m just saying that we could be the Black Creek ghost detectives. We can investigate hauntings and paranormal activity around the village.”

I thought about Angus’ idea for a minute. It was interesting. Even if we weren’t serious, it was fun to imagine it.

“What would we call ourselves?” I asked.

“What about JAM Ghost Detectives?” Angus said. “JAM stands for Jamie, Angus, and Maggie?”

Maggie turned up her nose. “That’s no good, Angus! Jam goes on toast. No, it should be named after Jamie since none of this would have happened without him. It should have at least part of his name in it. Hey, what about Cornelius?”

“No Cornelius!” I protested.

“Who is Cornelius?” Angus asked.

“He was my grandfather. Cornelius is my middle name,” I said.

“Cool,” Angus said and went back to licking his ice cream that had started to drip onto the cone.

“I’ve got it!” Maggie said. “Jamie C. O’Hare–Ghosts Beware. It rhymes!

"Catchy," I said. "I like it."

"It works. We can add Paranormal Investigators to the full name," Angus added.

"Then it's settled," I said, but I didn't think it wouldn't amount to anything.

"Hey! Look up there," Maggie said. "Why is smoke coming out of the chimney at the toy factory?"

"Yeah, that's strange," Angus said. "That place has been empty for years!"

I saw the plumes of black smoke above the large brick building in the distance. "Didn't Sydney say something about the toy factory on her blog?" I asked.

As we got closer to the building, my eyes were drawn to a light flickering deep inside, but visible through the windows. A familiar chill went down my spine.

"Did anyone see that light?" I asked.

"I did, and I'm suddenly freezing!" Maggie said.

"I didn't see anything!" Angus said, scrambling for his phone.

Maggie and I gave each other a knowing look.

"Jaaaaammmmiiieeee… Jaaaammmmmieeeeee ..."

"Here we go again!" I said.

THE END

Write a Review

C. Wade Jacobs would love to hear what you thought of her book. Authors use those reviews to improve their next book. You can leave your review on monkeybarbooks.com. If you're under 13, please ask an adult to help you.

We would be thrilled if you could post your review on Amazon or on your preferred online bookstore. The more we hear from you, the easier it is for others to find this book.
And be careful not to give away any of the surprises in the story. Let's make sure readers can enjoy their new book!

Thank you!

About the Author

C. Wade Jacobs has been creating characters and stories in her imagination since she was a child. She finally decided the write them down and share them with the world. She lives in Ottawa, Ontario Canada with her son, their Boston Terrier and Devon Rex cat.

More Kid Reviews

The protagonist Jamie moves to Black Creek expecting to just find a quiet, boring town, but that's not in the cards for Jamie C. O'Hare. Instead, he stumbles upon an age-old mystery, ghosts, and possibly, some friends. This fast-paced mystery is guaranteed to get your heart racing. It deserves 5 stars.

~ Kiana H.

I am not normally the reading type but this is a 5 star book. I can relate to Maggie because my two best friends are boys like Janie and Angus. The mystery and adventures are very exhilarating and anticipating. I very much love Jamie's sister Janine. She is probably my favorite character. She is such a material girl, I love her personality. This book is a page turner, I hope you guys like this book when you read it!

~ Fiona F.

I would give this book 4 stars because it is fast paced and not boring. It has some comedy, some action and some adventure. I love this book and I think that the author should definitely write more books.

~ Clare M.

I would give it 5 stars, because it's a nice book and a funny book. I would read more books, because these are cool books.

~ Ashwin S.

I enjoyed this book because of how the author can get what we 12-13 kids like or think is funny in a book and still can get a great and exciting story. I would recommend this book to anybody between the ages of 12 to 13 just because of how the author is not only able to write an interesting story but also put gen z humor in it.

~ CHARLIE